THE METHODS OF
TALENT
AND
POTENTIAL

The Breaking of Old Psychological Barriers.

by MARQUIS "POOH" DUNN

The Methods of Talent and Potential

Pres.tig.ious Publications

Copyright 2021 by Marquis "Pooh" Dunn

Dedications

I dedicate this book to my family, friends and loved ones; you mean the world to me! And in loving memories to Jerry O Lewis… You'll never be forgotten my brother… Rest peacefully homie.

Acknowledgements

First and foremost, I would like to thank my Lord and Savior, Jesus Christ for blessing me with the ability to formulate, construct, and create, the perfect story, from my perspective. Every word that I was able to use, honestly, came from the many prayers that I constantly prayed, before writing this book, especially, while being incarcerated.

I would like to thank all of my love ones, both living and deceased. You may be gone physically but, spiritually, you'll never be forgotten, and will forever live on in each of our hearts – and this book is a true testament of that.

I would like to thank my mother Mrs. Jacqueline Dunn-Clayborn, my three-beautiful daughter's Marquisia S. Dunn, Marquisa L. Dunn and Destinee' N. Dunn, and my two grandsons Kayce & Armani Dunn.

Last but not least, I would like to thank Ms. Latoya McCrary, who listened to every thought, idea, and was definitely my biggest supporter in writing this book. You always made time through your many visits, phone-calls, and letters to give me the constructive feedback that I needed in order to complete this book. Thank you!

To my editor, Donna Christopher, thank you for your help with completing this book. And thank you, Tim Dawson, for my book cover. You both are truly appreciated for everything you have done to help make this book come together.

P.S. Shot out to all my brothers who were on lockdown with me, who took time out of their busy days to listen to my constant rambling about the chapters planned for my book. From Hardeman County all the way to Riverbend Maximum Security Prison, you know who you are. And you know that it's nothing but love my brothers and I mean that! "Through God, all things are possible," and to me, this completed project definitely proves that.

Tee, we're on our way my brother. Hopefully, you will enjoy the book cover...

THE METHODS OF
TALENT
AND
POTENTIAL

The breaking of old psychological barriers

Introduction

Family – A group of people connected by blood or marriage sharing common ancestry.

Love – Intense affection for another arising out of kinship or personal ties.

Loyalty – Faithful in allegiance to one's country or government; faithful to a person/people, cause, idea or custom.

Jealousy – suspicious or fearful of being replaced by a rival; resentful or bitter in rivalry.

Deception – the act of deceiving; the factor state of being deceived; anything which deceives or deludes.

Betrayal – to be disloyal; unfaithful; to indicate; to deceive.

All the above describe the elements of the Clifton family. And the question is, are they strong enough to overcome? Or will it completely destroy them entirely. Inquiring minds want to know.

Chapter 1

It was an incredibly wonderful and beautiful day of June something. The year was nineteen seventy something. A stupendously attractive goddess of a woman was finally coming into her own, unknowingly.

The unseen powers that were responsible for all of life's existence was transitioning her in a way that she couldn't possibly believe. But, as time passed, she would slowly begin to understand.

Her name is, Survivor. I call her this because, from the very beginning of her life here on earth, that's exactly what she has done. "Survive."

Life was tough for Survivor. But somehow, she always managed to make a way for herself. She built a mental strength inside of her that could not be denied. One that she would claim as her very own doing at first, only because she was blatantly unaware of the true presence that was really responsible for molding her. That presence being God, "The Father" Himself.

Survivor was a phenomenal woman by all means and very easy on the eyes. Although she birth two children, and was a single-parent mom, the men adored her.

Her dark, milk chocolate colored smooth skin, doe-like eyes, full-sized lips, and her chiseled frame was a complete magnet for the opposite sex. And she knew it. On top of that, she had the confidence, class, and sex appeal to match.

Although these strong characteristic traits made her extremely desirable by many men, they also caused her to be envied as well.

But enough about Survivor for the current moment. Instead, let us place our attention on her children – Talent and Potential. Two very unique children that would eventually be led down two different paths only to end up at the same destination in the end. Victory and Restoration.

Talent was a very strong willed and highly intelligent individual with a vision as broad as the sea. The genius of the family some would even say. She had a caramel color skin tone that was slightly lighter than her mother's complexion. With the same doe-like eyes and full-size lips as well. Her eyes held a slight slant to them, like that of an Asian, giving her a very distinctive look. Even exceeding the normalcy in which she's currently being described.

Talent was absolutely beautiful in the simplest of ways. She had something very special about herself. Something that would eventually cause her to be envied in a very profound way as well. Even by those closest to her, just as they had done her mother.

But, unlike Survivor, who basked in the attention of others, whether positive or negative, Talent would humbly shy away from it all. Her quiet demeanor gave her the appearance of being shy to those that didn't know her in which she would later use to her advantage.

Talent minimized her words for a reason. She learned at a very early age that the less you spoke, and the more you actually listened, the more information you were able to obtain. And obtain information she did.

Sometimes she would ease drop on the adult conversations that were shared between Grandma Clifton, and several other members of her household, while lying amongst them pretending to be asleep. These conversations gave her an added advantage that she already held over children her same age by giving her the ability to know more, see more, and understand life more, even as a child.

Although, Talent was somewhat of an introvert in public, when it came to matters of right and wrong, she was a very outspoken person. And once again, like her mother, full of confidence.

She was never afraid to speak the truth about the things that really mattered most to her. And for the few times that she spoke her truth, it was done with such a maturity that even the adults were impressed.

But this wasn't Talent's battle. The qualities spoken about Talent are only a few of her strength's. Although she had many incredible strengths about her, it was her weaknesses that concerned her most.

Weaknesses that caused her to become a completely different individual, especially when she was provoked. And Talent despised this weakness she knew she had.

When upset, Talent's anger was expressed in a violent manner that was sometimes uncontrollable, even for her. She never liked fighting, but she left many scars and bruises on those she had to quarrel with. Both mentally and physically. Her anger, and the violence from it, was the reason why she prayed so hard.

She needed God to help her with her anger before it completely destroyed her entire life. When it came to her violent temper, she was a terrible mixture of her great grandmother, Grandma Clifton, her grandmother, Mrs. B. Lee, and her mother, Survivor. Three beautifully spirited women that held a no-nonsense attitude when it came to foolishness.

Although, the women in Talent's family were beautiful, intelligent, and very sexy, they were also dangerous and could be very conniving as well. And Talent received a triple dosage of these highly unwarranted gifts, in which she would in time recognize as she matured and grew into the intelligent young woman she was.

Because her inherited gifts would eventually lead her into a very prominent position of power, someday. One that she had unknowingly craved since she was a small child.

Chapter 2

Potential was born on June something, nineteen seventy something, at Meharry Hospital in the beautiful city of Nashville, TN. It was a happy day for Miss Survivor Clifton.

Potential's Father, showing no interest in wanting to be a part of his young son's life, abandoned them from the very moment that Potential was conceived. He left Survivor with the responsibility of raising their child all on her own, which she would definitely do to the best of her ability.

Potential was a strong and healthy child. At birth he weighed ten pounds and something, while stretching twenty something odd inches in length. His size and strength would be a much-needed asset for him in the years to come, due to all the many obstacles that he would face throughout his life.

He had the same caramel complexion as his older sister Talent, with the same slanted eyes as well. Although they both had different father's, they still resembled one another tremendously. It could honestly be said that their mother must have had a thing for lighter men.

Either way, it all worked out perfectly in the sight of the Lord, because He blessed her with two amazingly beautiful children.

From the very moment that Potential was born, there was a uniqueness about him. An unusual oddity that could be seen with the naked eye, by both the doctor and family alike. It was even said that the blind knew it as well.

After signing the release papers for her and her son to be discharged, Survivor was wheeled to the patient pick-up area where she waited for her father to pull the car around, so they could finally go home. Three days in the hospital was more than enough for her. She could not wait to lay down in her own bed.

Just the thought of being back at home with her new baby caused a little anxiety to well up within her. She had to take a few deep breaths in order to calm herself.

As she sat at the curve-side, cradling her son, patiently waiting for her father to turn the corner, several individuals passed her heading to and from the hospital. "Just another typical day at Meharry," she assumed, speaking out loud. She was glad that she was finally leaving.

As Big John rounded the corner in his huge Sedan heading in his daughter's direction, something extremely odd caught Survivor's eye.

It was a blind couple being led towards the hospital's entrance by what seemed to be either their daughter or a very close relative. She assumed a relative due to the striking resemblance that each of them shared. They were visiting Meharry for the very first time for their monthly eye exams.

Although blind, the couple was preparing themselves to undergo a very serious series of surgeries that could possibly grant them with the ability to see for the very first time in their lives. And, Meharry Hospital, although black owned and also majority black staffed, was the place in which they had chosen to perform their surgery.

Their decision caused a lot of controversy throughout the entire city of Nashville amongst the local whites. It was vehemently protested due to the racial indifference and the so-called color line that so blatantly existed in the south during that time.

But, neither T. Thomas nor did Mrs. Ida B. McCreary ever concern themselves with the ignorance that surrounded them. They simply made the choice that best suited them and their needs - and Meharry was it.

To them, it wasn't about race at all. It was about proficiency. And from the many arduous hours of research that they both conducted on the matter, they discovered that Meharry carried one of the best ophthalmologists in the entire southern region at the time. Furthermore, solidifying their decision regardless of who liked it or not.

So, as they continuously made their way toward the hospital's main entrance, a strange and very peculiar feeling entered Mrs. Ida B's body, jolting her completely. She made an abrupt stop as if she had been suddenly overcome by some form of paralysis, causing her daughter's arm to jerk backwards harshly.

She faced her daughter and asked incredulously with an extremely puzzled look plastered upon her face, "by any chance, is there a child present somewhere in the vicinity?" Her question caused her daughter Dorothy to become curious as to why she asked.

As she stammered over her words, while scanning the area once again, Dorothy nervously replied, "Yes ma'am, there is. But why would you ask that?" Her eyes landed on the woman in which they had just passed, busily rocking her child. "Mother, what's wrong? Should I go get help?" she asked waiting for a reply. But when she didn't immediately receive one, she continued to question her mother. "What is it? Mother... Please, talk to me!" Dorothy pleaded, showing genuine concern.

Mrs. Ida B. gently began patting her daughter's hand in an attempt to calm her down. She had obviously become frantic, and Mrs. Ida didn't need that. She assured her everything was fine before calmly explaining the feelings she received just as they were entering the hospital's corridor.

After easing her daughter's nerves, she soothingly asked her next question, "Dorothy, was there any way that you could determine whether the child that the woman was holding in her arms was a male or female?"

"No ma'am, I could not," she solemnly replied before adding, "but, the blanket covering the child was blue. So, the baby could possibly be a boy."

Upon that information Mrs. Ida then insisted on being introduced to the mother of the child herself.

"Take me to her, please," Mrs. Ida B. asked in somewhat of a stern manner.

This statement brought Dorothy's nervousness back full fledge for the second time in less than a few short minutes. She swallowed deeply and skeptically asked her mother, "Are you sure that's a good idea?" She curiously surveyed the massive sea of black faces that currently surrounded them at the moment.

"Of course, it's a good idea, honey. Now, stop worrying and do for me what I've asked of you." Mrs. Ida B spoke to her with slight authority as she smiled at her to help dissipate the tension that she felt was restricting her child from moving forward.

Although, still very skeptical and extremely leery of her surroundings, Dorothy complied with her mother's request and hesitantly approached Survivor just as she was loading her son into the vehicle.

"Excuse me. Excuse me, Miss," Dorothy said timidly, barely loud enough for her to hear. She walked closer to Survivor, shortening the distance between them by a few inches.

Feeling of an unknown presence, that someone was now standing behind her, Survivor made a quick pivoting move placing herself on the balls of her feet. She was prepared to strike as she came face to face with a woman that she had never seen before.

Dorothy's green eyes penetrated Survivor's soul deeply, startling her in a most profound way. But before any response could be made on her behalf, the strange woman spoke once again. "I'm so sorry if I startled you, ma'am, and if I've caused you any type of discomfort, I truly apologize."

Survivor carefully studied her with the precision of a lioness. Looking her up and down, while constantly keeping her distance, just in case things got a little weird between them.

Sensing the awkwardness of the situation, Dorothy politely introduced herself by extending her hand, as if to say, *I come in peace.* "Hi, I'm Dorothy McCreary, and these two-beautiful people are my parents, Mr. T. Thomas and Mrs. Ida B. McCreary," she respectfully said. She pointed from one to the other as she spoke their names. "If it's not too much to ask of you, my mother would like a few moments of your time, please. I told her that I didn't think that it was a good idea for us to approach you like this, but she insisted." Dorothy said apologetically.

Survivor watched the woman as the words escaped her mouth with an intense caution written all over her face. She made it very obvious to her that she didn't trust them.

Big John did the same exact thing while exiting the driver's seat of his huge sedan making his way to his daughter's side.

Seeing this reaction from them and also acknowledging their resistance to what she had spoken just moments prior, Dorothy felt the need to further explain the situation a little more in depth, in hopes that they would fully understand, possibly allowing her mother to take over from there.

"My parents are some very spiritual people, and as you can tell, they're also blind," Dorothy stated. She was trying her best to keep Survivor's undivided attention and help alleviate some of the doubt that she saw within her before continuing. "At times, my mother receives these amazing notions, in which are very seldom ever wrong. And today, she believes she has just received one that possibly concerns your child," Dorothy stated, pausing to catch her breath before asking her main question. "After all, your baby is a boy correct?" she said matter-of-factly looking into Survivor's eyes.

Upon hearing the mention of her child's gender spoken to her by a stranger, Survivor's body language became as aggressive as the loud rattling sound of a venomous rattlesnake who was about to attack. Her eyes squinted into tight small slits, peering dangerously at Dorothy with an immense coldness.

Big John, feeling the aggression exuding from his daughter's body, gently placed a comforting hand on her shoulder, assuring her that everything was okay.

"Calm down, baby girl, and just hear them out," he said whispering into his daughter's ear as he stepped forward. He slightly placed himself in front of Survivor to keep her from lashing out, and for the first time, making his presence fully known.

Lord, you know my heart, and you know that we don't want any trouble, Big John silently prayed. *But, if these people attempt to try anything foolish, then forgive me, Lord, for what I might have to do to them... Because, I'm definitely not having it!* He was being sincere as he prepared to squash the innocent looking trio, that he thought could possibly be a threat to his family.

Unaware of the current thoughts that truly ramshacked Big John's mind at the time, Dorothy aimlessly proceeded on with her message. And after hearing her out, while carefully evaluating her every word as attentively as a homicide detective on the hunt for his murderer, he realized that they were completely genuine. He leaned inside the car, removed his grandson from his car seat, who was still covered with the blanket, and slightly inched it away from his handsome face. Proudly, he showed the McCreary's his grandchild.

Dorothy was absolutely amazed at the strong features of the child and how well they all meshed together. *I have never before seen such simple features connect together so beautifully*, she thought to herself.

Potential's thick eyebrow's along with his extremely lengthy eyelashes accentuated his slanted brown eyes perfectly. Just as his broad cheekbones did the same exact thing with his luscious full-sized lips.

Dorothy vividly described the strength in the child's appearance to her mother and father. Instantaneously, a huge smile graced their faces. Especially Big John's, for he saw nothing but pure strength and true potential in his grandson's slanted eyes.

Full of elation, the couple then earnestly prayed for Survivor and her child. Assuring her that not only was her son a blessing from God, but that he would also be a blessing to many others as well, as long as she kept him on the right path.

Survivor sat quietly, while listening to Mrs. Ida B. McCreary as she constantly spoke, wondering what it all meant. As if reading her mind, Mrs. Ida began speaking yet again looking directly into Survivor's direction, "This child has the potential of becoming a very great man in his lifetime. But it will solely be based on the decisions that he will make for himself as he constantly matures." Her tone was firm, and she spoke with a serious look upon her face. "Especially the decisions of his future," she finalized while caressing the small fragile hand of the baby with her thumb.

Hearing her son's name spoken by this mysterious blind woman of Caucasian descent, Survivor instantly began questioning herself as to how she actually knew the things in which she did. *How does this woman know my son's name? Did I tell her? Of course, I didn't. I've barely said much of anything at all.* Question after question constantly absorbed her mind, leaving her completely flabbergasted.

Dumbfounded and slightly confused by her current events, Survivor finally stammered out the question that she had been wanting to ask since Mrs. Ida B. McCreary first began to speak. Catching her at an appropriate time in between sentences, she did exactly that. "Excuse me, Mrs. McCreary. But, how did you know that my son's name was Potential?" Survivor asked boldly, even though that was not her intentions. She caught Mrs. Ida off guard.

Pondering for a second or two on the question that she had been asked, Mrs. Ida kindly replied, "Sweetheart, I had no idea that was his name at all. What I merely said was that he has the potential of becoming a very great man in this lifetime." She politely reiterated to Survivor, before continuing. "But, since that is his name, it truly fits him well. My darling, the Lord has revealed to me deep within my spirit, on this most wonderful and glorious day, that He has a great plan already worked out pertaining to your son."

Mrs. Ida B. made that last statement before quoting the scriptures of Jeremiah 33:3 combined with a little bit of Jeremiah 29:11 to Survivor. "Call unto me and I will answer you, and show you great and mighty things, which you do not know. For I know the thoughts that I think toward you, says the Lord. Thoughts of peace and not of evil, to give you a future and a hope."

Mrs. Ida B found Survivor's hand, held it tenderly within her grasp, and gently said, "Now, if you take heed to things in which I've just shared with you, and follow these words from the Lord, your son will be a blessing to everyone that crosses his path. Go against them, and he will be an absolute burden to all that know him... Especially to you my darling, especially to you."

And with that being said, the McCreary's walked away just as pleasantly as they had done when they approached Survivor. Never once looking back again.

A tear fell from Survivor's eye as she watched the McCreary's slowly fade into the midst of the crowd. For the first time in her young life, she earnestly prayed thanking her Heavenly Father for blessing her with her children. "Lord, I promise to do all that I can to guide them on the right path and to protect them from the ugliness of this world." She honestly and sincerely prayed. "According to your ways and with your help of course... Even if it cost me my very own life. In Jesus precious name, I pray...Amen!"

Survivor, then climbed into the car with her father, and they pulled away from the curb. All the while looking into the backseat at her sleeping child silently thinking, *you will definitely be a blessing baby boy... You will definitely be a blessing.* She then closed her eyes, resting her head upon the headrest of her seat, drifting off into a peaceful sleep as well.

Chapter 3

Things were peaceful in the Clifton home. Or should I say, as peaceful as any inner-city ghetto home could possibly be.

Although, the house was filled to capacity, and at times, food was a very scarce commodity, their home was full of love, loyalty, and true family devotion. This bond caused them to be one of the most popular families on the entire west side of Nashville.

What the Clifton's lacked in material assets, they surely made up for with integrity, honor, principles, and morals. Establishing within them a richness that couldn't be denied by anyone that knew them. Especially their neighbors.

The Clifton's were a very genuine group of people. A people of good character, strong work ethic and strict discipline. And they lived their lives accordingly, each and every member. They believed in giving everyone, known or unknown to them, more than their fair share of love and respect. But, on the flip side of things, attracted their appointed share of trouble, if you crossed the line. Depending on the person and their actions. To them this was more than justifiable due to the fact that they were such kind people.

They knew that love overpowered hate by all means and preferred it more than anything. But they also knew that at times you had to beat the devil out of some folks as well. This was necessary in order to teach a lesson and bring a certain type of clarity into a situation, as they sometimes seemed to occur.

Like the time when Grandma Clifton, Talent, and Potential's great grandmother caught wind that her husband at the time, who was Mrs. B. Lee's father, was sneaking around with a relative of one of her close friends.

Now Grandma Clifton, who was normally known for her very respectful mannerism, loving spirit, and very soft-spoken words, could easily transform and show a different side of herself. Especially when provoked, or when people so blatantly tried to play her for a fool or had the tendency of taking her kindness for weakness.

And on this particular day, that's exactly what her ex-husband tried to do. Either play her for a fool or depict her as some type of weakling. But in either case, he had her sadly mistaken. Out of all the women in the world, he should've actually known better than to play with Grandma Clifton.

Yes, she had changed her life tremendously for the sake of her family. And yes, she had traded in all of her clubbing, drinking, and fighting days for long church services, big hats, and daily scripture readings. Up until that point, all her changed ways had truly done her a lot of good.

But, as hard as she tried, and as strong as her faith and her walk had become in Christ Jesus, she just couldn't allow these two idiots to get away with this blatant act of betrayal.

The devil had finally found a soft spot in her armor, and he seized the moment with gladness. No matter how many times she recited Ephesians 6, verses eleven through seventeen, nothing seemed to work. And although the word of God clearly states, *to be angry, but sin not*, Grandma Clifton couldn't bring herself to follow that commandment. So, she repented several times before actually heading out her front door, asking God for his forgiveness. "Lord, forgive me now for what I'm about to do... In Jesus name I pray." She kept right on walking without a second thought.

The temper that she had buried deep within so many odd years ago resurfaced and reared its ugly head once again. *Why won't people just let you be a good person!* she thought to herself while shaking her head from disappointment as her anger bubbled up inside of her like the lava of a volcano that was about to erupt.

She tried humbling herself by talking herself down, trying to let it go completely. But her pride just wouldn't allow her to do so. *Grandma Clifton could not, and most definitely would not tolerate this type of infidelity from anyone!* she thought. *Not from my spouse, and especially not from the cousin of one of my closest friends either.* She proceeded, knowing that it could possibly sever the relationship between her and her good friend Rubie forever.

"Well, if our friendship ends over this, then, so be it," she stubbornly said out loud. "I am nobody's fool, and never will I be!" She yelled her frustrations angrily.

Her pride was on the line now, and it had blocked out all rational thinking on her behalf. So, with nothing but pure rage in her heart, and her love one's infidelity constantly bombarding her brain, she discarded the straight-edged razor blade with the pearl handle for her 12-gauge shotgun and set out on her mission of finding the two disloyal varmints that deserved as many buck shots as their deceitful behinds could possibly hold. And she had every intention of giving each of them more than their full share of lead as soon as she crossed their paths.

Without a car, or the ability to drive, Grandma Clifton struck out on foot, walking as fast as her swollen feet could carry her.

She was seven and a-half-months pregnant at the time, and still moving with the agility of a gazelle. Swiftly and smoothly. She switched her shotgun from shoulder to shoulder every few steps as if she were performing some type of military drill.

Several neighbors, along with a few kind-hearted strangers that noticed her face but didn't actually know her personally, pulled alongside her showing genuine concern and tried to convince her that whatever it was that she was about to do, or even thinking of doing, wouldn't be worth it. But she paid them no mind.

Some even prayed for her out loud in hopes that their words would register that way. She simply acknowledged them with nothing more than a nodding of her head. But without any eye-contact, she continued on with her stroll. Never missing a beat.

The mere mention of God conflicted Grandma Clifton spirit tremendously. It was as if He was actually speaking to her Himself as scriptures consistently flooded her mind and wouldn't relent. But she didn't allow that to deter her either.

Scriptures like, *be angry but sin not, nor give place to the devil.* But the one that reverberated through her brain most of all was Ephesians 4: verses thirty-one and thirty-two. Which clearly told her, *let all bitterness, wrath, anger, clamor, and all evil speaking be put away from you, with all malice – and to be kind, tenderhearted, forgiving one another as God in Christ forgave you.*

As bad as she wanted to abide by the word of God at that time, she just couldn't bring herself to do it. So, she ignored it and kept right on moving. Even more adamant now in reaching her destination than she had been before.

For the life of her, she couldn't understand why God would even be placing those types of things on her mind at the time. Especially when being kind, forgiving and not sinning were totally out of the question for her at the moment. As a matter of fact, she had every intention of doing the exact opposite of those things, and sinning was at the top of her list.

She thought about all that God had forgiven her for. Some things she knew she shouldn't have been forgiven for. And yes, she knew that He had renewed her tremendously. But Grandma Clifton said she wasn't God! She was nothing more than a sinner. And if He had forgiven her once, then He would definitely do it again, she reasoned. Because there was no way on His green earth, that she was allowing this disrespectful act of betrayal to stand!

She double-checked her shotgun, making sure that it was prepared for action. Realizing that it was, she picked up her pace, trying her best to make it to Dell Way Villa Apartments as quickly as she possibly could.

Grandma Clifton walked for more than an hour and forty-five minutes, when she finally made it to the busy intersection of Trinity Lane and Dickerson Rd. She was now only a short distance from the cousin's home. Although she was exhausted, and her feet and ankles had swollen twice their original size, her anger and determination steadily propelled her forward.

As Grandma Clifton rounded the corner, passing the local convenient store that sat on the end of the street, only a couple blocks from her destination, she spotted the loving duo as they were exiting the market with what seemed to be a bag full of groceries. She said, "Lady Luck must be on my side. Or was it the wiles of the devil aligning things so that they could work out in his favor with his many lies." Grandma Clifton considered. "Oh… this is the reason why the money has been so tight lately huh?" She angrily spat, inching closer and closer to them with every step.

They were laughing and carrying on like they hadn't a care in the world. Not knowing that danger was easing upon them as quietly as a lioness who was stalking her prey.

As she came within firing range of the couple, standing no more than fifteen feet away, she finally locked eyes with her husband who instantly froze in his tracks.

His body stiffened as if he was paralyzed from the neck down, drawing the attention of the woman he was with, causing her to look up as well. As soon as she realized who stood before her, her knees instantly buckled from underneath her and perspiration seeped from her pores by the pint, instantly causing her to become fatigued. Nervousness seized her body, causing her entire frame to uncontrollably convulse with fear.

As Grandma Clifton leveled the gun at her husband's chest. The sound words of Solomon in Ecclesiastes 7, verses eight and nine, slowly entered her mind. *The end of a thing is better than it's beginning; the patient in spirit, is better than the proud in spirit. Do not hasten in your spirit to be angry, for anger rest in the bosom of fools.*

And although she had used this scripture several different times in her past, in order to help alleviate her anger, all she was able to comprehend from it on this day was, *the end of a thing is better than it's beginning...* and she pulled the trigger.

"BOOM!

The innocent bystanders that stood around watching the incident unfold scattered like roaches once they heard the sounds of the loud explosion. Once the smoke cleared, the couple lay sprawled out on the pavement drenched in a thick, gooey, red substance, that definitely appeared to be blood.

Piercing screams echoed loudly throughout the area as people frantically ran, searching and yelling for help!

The scene was so chaotic that no one actually witnessed the traumatized couple clumsily scramble to their feet and high-tail around the corner of the store. Running as fast as their scared little legs could carry them. Leaving behind the car, and everything else that they had with them.

As Grandma Clifton pulled herself from off of the pavement after being knocked down from the powerful blowback of the shotgun blast, she wondered to herself how she could've possibly missed. Especially after she had gotten so close to them before firing her weapon.

Then just like that, it dawned on her, she had an awakening moment. The reason she had not hit them, was because it was never a part of God's plan to bring harm to them, so she figured. He was merely showing her those things, so she could actually move on and finally let him go. The bible clearly states that, *a man devises many plans in his heart, but it's God's plan that stands in the end.*

In the end it was definitely his plan that prevailed. Meaning that, no matter if we like it or not, God's purpose for our lives would be fulfilled. Especially for those that are called. Grandma Clifton had definitely been called and she knew it.

She thanked God once again for protecting her in all her ignorance and stubbornness. She discarded the shotgun in a near-by trash bend, and she vowed to never disobey God's word ever again. And right at that very moment for her, a euphoric feeling of warmness encompassed her entire body from head to toe. So much so that she could actually feel its warmness escaping her body from deep within and running down her legs.

Grandma Clifton's water had broken – and several hours after that, Mrs. B. Lee finally pushed her way into the world without a sound. She was looking around with the attentiveness and fearlessness of a true Clifton female in the making.

Chapter 4

Life passed by swiftly for the Clifton family. But it all went unnoticed until someone began to reminisce. There were four generations of Clifton women now. And to Grandma Clifton, it seemed just like yesterday that her water broke at the scene of that local convenient store, the same day that she gave birth to Mrs. B. Lee, who later gave birth to Survivor after marrying Big John. And then at the tender age of seventeen, very much still a child herself, Survivor gave birth to Talent. Followed by Potential several years later.

God blessed each of these women with a very profound role in their family's history, and the ability to spread it from one generation to the next for many years to come. But it was now time for Talent to receive her fair share of their lineage, from each perspective role these women play in their family's life.

This responsibility only enhanced Talent's intelligence and allowed her to surpass majority of the children her same age and older, along with some adults, in common knowledge by far.

There were times, even at a very young age, that she literally held full-fledged conversations with the older adults of her household about real life circumstances, or just everyday issues. Things that it seemed she shouldn't have known anything about, but she did. Topics that ranged from politics and religion, all the way down to American History. Especially African American history which she loved.

Educating herself about her people only strengthened her young mind even more. Broadening her horizons in a very surmountable way. From traveling the world through the pages of her reading material, Talent realized that she could be a lot more than just some ordinary inner-city kid that resided on the west side of Nashville.

And women such as Harriet Tubman, Rosa Parks, Lena Horne, Althea Gibson, Maya Angelou, Angela Davis, Fannie Lou Hamer, and many, many more had shown her this firsthand from the success that they all had encountered during their lifetimes.

Her studies stretched from slavery to politics, from politics to theater, and from theater and music to sports. Not to mention African-America literature, which was responsible for giving America some of its most creative stories, all based off of hundreds of years of suffering. Stories by amazing author's such as Langston Hughes, Carter G. Woodson, Richard Wright, Ralph Ellison, and James Baldwin, only to name a few.

The more information that Talent received, the keener her mind became, and the more she began to truly realize that knowledge really was powerful.

She witnessed this power through the incredible women that she read about in books. Especially when it came to women like Fannie Lou Hamer who had risen and found her voice, and in doing so, she articulated, motivated, and inspired the aspiration of millions of her fellow black Americans. But she could also see the same power in the women that were currently raising her. And because of this, she couldn't wait to influence the mind of her little brother. He would be her first student.

Fannie Lou Hamer became a very powerful woman despite the fact that she was born and raised as a sharecropper in the terrible, poverty-stricken area of the Mississippi Delta, was the twentieth child of all her parents' children, and dropped out of school completely at the age of twelve. She possessed the knowledge needed to accomplish everything she did in life. She became one of the most powerful political forces of her decade many years later. So much so, that her name became internationally known all across the world.

And to Talent, that was more than enough determination for her to rise above the norm and always do her greatest, in which she would not be denied.

Now she understood why Big John and her grandmother, Mrs. B. Lee, always made such a big deal about exceeding the limits of her education. Especially since both of them were basically forced to drop out of school around the same age that Fannie Lou Hamer herself quit, only for her to do some of the same menial tasks that farm life consisted of, in which they also severely disliked. But they had no other choice in the matter at the time due to their circumstances.

Mrs. B. Lee and Big John prided themselves on being hard workers. From a very early age, working hard was all they had ever known to do. Regardless of how much they may have enjoyed school back then, it was never much of an option for either to finish. But what was an option was for them to help put food on their families table. And every able-bodied person was needed in order for their family to survive.

And survive they had done for many years despite the cruel and arduous days of their upbringing. Although the struggle hadn't completely subsided for them as a family, they had more than learned to adjust, adapt, and maintain their survival firsthand.

As a family, they knew that one day they would annihilate the horrific strongholds of African American poverty completely. Starting with Talent, who was most definitely sought to be somewhat of a genius. Never before, out of all of their years of living on God's green earth, had anyone in their family ever seen someone that made everything that they had ever done look so simple. Until Talent. And to her, it was.

Her academic skills were so astounding that the metro school board of education advanced her two grade levels higher, taking her from fourth grade to sixth. They also placed her in all distinguished honors classes in order to challenge her levels of advancement. But even that didn't work.

After a week or so of filling out her new courses and getting better acquainted with the curriculum, Talent excelled in that as well. She answered questions as if she was a jeopardy contestant or something, tapping her desk and instantly blurting out the answers as they entered her mind.

There were even times where more than a few of her teachers would purposely misinform the class about certain things, just to see who would catch it. And as always, Talent did. She would politely raise her hand, ask for permission to approach the desk, and kindly whisper the correct answer into the teacher's ear, as if not to embarrass them. Then, gingerly return back to her seat as if nothing had happened leaving a huge smile plastered across the teacher's face.

Witnessing her humility and acknowledging the fact that she was so well informed about so many different things, made her teacher's love her even more. Talent instantly became one of their favorites. So much so that most of them had unintentionally began showing favoritism towards her.

Anytime a question was posed toward the class, normally it was Talent that they called upon in order to answer it. And she would always answer them correctly. This stirred up many different emotions amongst her fellow classmates, both positive and negative, which were outwardly expressed toward her daily.

There were a few students that disliked the fact that she was so intelligent, feeling as if she was a show-off. And these students did everything within their power to let her know how they felt verbally. They would call her names such as the teacher's pet and mocking her whenever she began to speak.

Knowing that it all stemmed from jealousy on their behalf, Talent never allowed the childish antics of their behavior to faze her one bit. She fully understood a few of the methods in which Satan had tried to use in order to keep her people from truly reaching their God appointed destiny's. Methods such as jealousy, envy, strife, fear, ignorance, laziness, and doubt.

And acknowledging this, she promised herself to always stay cognizant of the many pitfalls, traps and snares that would constantly be placed before her in order to bring about failure. Not only in life, but in the classroom as well. Which for her, would soon be tested. The more friends Talent attained from her kind gestures and genuine beliefs, the deeper the resentment of her antagonist grew as did their disrespectful ways.

Talent did not like altercations nor conflicts of any kind. Most of the time, she simply avoided altercations as best as she possibly could. Her discipline only fueled the girl's ego even more, causing them to believe that Talent was afraid of them. Her being afraid was definitely the furthest thing from the truth, and in due time they would find this out for themselves, along with many more of their classmates.

Just as Grandma Clifton once told her, while sharing one of her many stories about her past, *sometimes you just might have to beat the devil out of a few folks in order for them to learn their lesson, and so that they may receive their blessing.* With that thought in mind, Talent answered her last and final question... correctly as usual.

Chapter 5

As Survivor watched and cared for her son, the more Mrs. Ida B. McCreary's words rang true.

The things that Potential was able to do at such a young age surprised even her, making her feel as if her child had truly been blessed by God. Never in her lifetime had she witnessed an infant do the things that Potential was doing. Things such as walk or speak his very first words at seven and a half months old.

She knew that her mother had been born around the same time, and although she arrived a month and a half early, she was still described as being a very healthy and fearless child. Grandma Clifton was extremely proud that her daughter entered into this world without shedding a single tear, showing all necessary signs that indicated she was prepared for whatever obstacles life would throw her way.

But Potential was different, and Survivor knew it. Everything about Potential's life up until that point had been very peculiar, and also mystifying including his first steps. She started to reminisce, remembering everything as if it had just happened yesterday...

One day, while Survivor and a few more of her relatives were having a conversation in the kitchen of her home as she prepared dinner for the family, Potential sat on a blanket on the living room floor not too far away. He was having the time of his young life as he played with an assortment of colorful toys, lots of building blocks and race cars.

Survivor looked on in amazement at her son as she continued cooking and talking to her family members. Reprimanding him from time to time for placing certain objects into his mouth.

As if fully understanding his mother's request, Potential would instantly remove the toy from his face and go back to playing. His reactions made it appear as if he was merely checking to see if he still held her undivided attention regardless of whatever else it was that she was doing. And of course, he always did.

Survivor loved her children dearly and was very protective of them. Some would even say that she was over-protective in a sense. Like a mother bear was toward her cubs. And her relatives knew this. Whenever they wanted to rile her up, or receive a good laugh at her expense, they would begin making jokes about her kids. Especially Potential who had not yet begun to crawl, although he was 7 and a half months. For a Clifton child, this was extremely unusual. Very unusual.

Survivor's relatives, knowing that she was a bit self-conscious because of this, decided to have a little fun with her. They secretly signaled one another while snickering amongst themselves behind Survivor's back, giving each other a heads-up on what they were about to do.

Survivor was completely oblivious to her family's plan. As they continued to snicker, they almost gave themselves away. They finally gathered themselves well enough to begin the assault.

As they bombarded Survivor with joke after joke about the laziness of her son, Survivor's anger gradually escalated, increasing more and more with each passing word. She tried her best to contain it but was losing that battle completely, and her family recognized it.

They laughed under their breath until the point of tears, gesturing to one another to peep Survivor's demeanor, while wondering how long it would actually take before she completely lost it. They figured they would get an even better laugh off of her once she finally did.

Full of fury and madder than a pack of hornet's whose nest had been tampered with, Survivor tightly gripped the long, metal, handle of her cooking utensil. Trying so desperately not to give into the anger that was building up inside of her as Potential sat close by continuously playing with his toys, looking up into his mother's scowling face, until finally making eye contact. Potential smiled.

With steam seeping from her pores, as her chest heaved up and down with her erratic breathing, Survivor somehow managed to muster up a smile back toward her son. All the while, thinking in her mind *If any one of these heifer's say another word about my baby, family or not, I'm whooping somebody's behind up in here, and I'm not playing!* She said these words to herself without actually realizing her level of anger.

Sensing his mother's distress, Potential dropped his toys and placed his palms onto the floor out in front of him as if he were about to crawl. Survivor and her relatives attentively watched with excitement, patiently awaiting her son's first move.

Several seconds had passed and all Potential had done was rock back and forth, while wobbling from side to side as if he were about to topple over. His actions caused Survivor's relatives to burst into a gut-wrenching fit of laughter.

Instantly going into attack mode, Survivor proceeded forward toward her cousins with a vengeance. But before she could reach them, Pat, who was now frantically pointing at Potential and clearly unable to speak, caused Survivor to divert her eyes back toward her son. Potential had finally gathered his feet underneath his chubby little legs well enough to push himself into an erect standing position.

All the women within the home howled with excitement, jumping up and down as they screamed at the top of their lungs.

"Look girl, look! He's standing up on his own," Pat finally yelled with much enthusiasm as they continued to celebrate and shout with glee.

Now standing on very shaky legs, Potential made eye contact with each one of his mother's relatives as if to say, "I heard all the jokes that you guys were making about me, and how upset my mother became because of it, so now I'll show you."

Potential looked towards Survivor and started walking to his mother on very steady legs. He stopped in front of her, while looking up into her beautiful face and said, "food momma," as he pointed to a large platter of chicken that was stacked high upon a plate, sitting in the center of the stove.

Acknowledging her son's words, and witnessing him walk, Survivor swooped Potential up into her arms and aggressively kissed him with joy, with tears streaming down her face.

She then turned to her family members, who sat just as dumbfounded as she had been, and began to gloat. "Not only did my baby take his first steps," she said, "but he also spoke, now what!" She screamed out in excitement before asking, "Now what do y'all low down heifers have to say?" She swirled her son around in circles, before planting another dozen or more kisses onto his elated face.

Potential, enjoying the affection that his mother was currently giving him at the moment, giggled several times expressing his joy. But before she could do or say anything more, he spoke up once again.

"Down momma," he said asking his mother to place him back onto the floor so that he could resume playing with his toys. A bit surprised by his gesture, she gladly obliged laughing to herself as she politely done so.

Looking around at his mother's relatives once more before calmly walking away, Potential smiled yet again showing them his only tooth. He found his original spot on the blanket and grabbed his favorite toy as if nothing had ever happened.

Snapping Survivor out of her daydreaming, Potential placed a soft, wet kiss onto his mother's cheek, as he handed her a sheet of paper that contained his scribbled art drawings.

She started smiling while hugging her son before he ran away. Survivor finally took a look at the portrait. Although her son couldn't really write or spell as of yet, Potential had somehow managed to create a heart with the word, "love" etched directly through its center in the midst of all the scribbled lines.

Survivor observed the drawing in pure astonishment, as Mrs. McCreary's words once again re-entered her mind.

"Your son will be blessed. And has the Potential of becoming a very great man for your family"

Survivor remembered her saying those words clear as day as she said a small prayer for her son's safety as he continuously grew, hoping that God heard her every word.

"Watch over my son Lord, send your angels and give them charge over him, to keep him and to guide him in all of his ways." She earnestly prayed, quoting Psalms 91:11, which had become one of her most favorite scriptures. Especially since the birth of her son.

Chapter 6

It was a new school year for Talent, and she was super excited about it. She had a lot of accomplishments the previous year and couldn't wait to see what God had in store for her with the new year.

Everything looked bigger to her as she walked through the doors of her new environment. Although she saw a few familiar faces from the year before sprinkled throughout the very cluttered hallways, she was mainly surrounded by strangers. The new faces actually made her a little bit nervous.

As she scanned the crowded area, Talent thought that everyone seemed so much bigger than she was, causing her to feel like a midget walking amongst giants in a sense.

But the exhilaration of it all was amazing to her, and she couldn't wait to share every single detail of her new experience with her family as soon as she got the opportunity to do so.

Now, it's time to handle business, she thought to herself. She asked a few of her fellow students for directions to the main office, and upon receiving it, Talent headed straight that way.

Locating the door and entering the office, she was greeted by a very attractive and well-dressed African

American woman by the name of Mrs. Nicole whom she quickly found out to be the school's principal.

Mrs. Nicole was extremely nice and very polite. She assisted Talent in every way she possibly could in order to help get her better acquainted with her new surroundings.

"Oh, I see that you're not one to shy away from challenges," Mrs. Nicole said, as she browsed at Talent's class schedule before handing it to her. Mrs. Nicole congratulated Talent on challenging her mind, assuring her in all confidence that she would do an exceptional job in each class. She then pushed back from her desk and stood to her feet, walked towards her office door, smiled, and politely stepped to her left so Talent could exit so that she could help assist her next awaiting student.

Talent thanked Mrs. Nicole for her encouraging words as she walked towards the exit. But before she could completely make it out the door, Mrs. Nicole called to her once again.

"Excuse me, Talent," Mrs. Nicole said.

Talent turned to properly address her new principal. "Yes ma'am," she modestly replied.

"Would you like for someone to show you to your locker, or to your first period classroom?"

Talent politely rejected the offer. "No ma'am, that won't be necessary. But I truly appreciate the offer. Talent responded with a smile of her own as she allowed the door to close behind her.

Entering the now almost empty hallway full of confidence, Talent knew in her heart that it was going to be another incredible school year for her. With her schedule still in her hand, she observed her classes and was more than pleased with each and every one of them.

Talent looked forward to acquiring as much knowledge as she possibly could consume from every course. Especially theater. She figured theater would finally give her the ability to express herself and act out all of her inner-most feelings. With the elation that came from that thought alone, Talent performed a full circular ballerina twirl right there in the center of the hallway, not caring who witnessed it.

She allowed the sensational feelings to thrive within her for a moment longer before finally composing herself and heading in the direction of her locker. She then placed all of the unnecessary items in her locker that she didn't need for her first period class.

Rummaging inside of her locker, Talent was folding up her class schedule, tucking it away in one of her class folders, when out of the blue someone called her name.

"Hey Talent," the familiar voice screamed.

She looked up scanning her surroundings but couldn't locate the face of the person in which she knew the voice belonged to, her big cousin Liz.

After several more seconds of searching, still unable to find her, the familiar voice called out yet again. "Hey Talent, over here girl!" Liz yelled. Standing in the midst of the crowd that was forming and surveying the area once more, Talent finally saw the waving arm of her big cousin Liz as it swayed back and forth. Liz was several yards away, almost at the end of the hallway.

Talent headed in Liz's direction with a huge smile plastered upon her face. She was anxious to give her cousin all of the early morning details of her first day. All of a sudden, she experienced a very harsh and neck jolting bump coming from her blind side, almost completely knocking Talent clean off her feet. This caused her to lose control and drop her books. She also bit into her tongue, sending a sharp, shrieking pain coursing throughout the inside of her mouth, almost causing her to curse. But she didn't let out a single word.

She looked around to see who was responsible for the disrespectful act. She knew in her heart that it was too hard of a bump in order for it to be an accident.

Anger shot through Talent's body as she took a few deep breaths, trying her best to contain it. Her day had been going so well up until that point, and she wasn't about to let it be ruined by some idiot. As she diligently worked on pushing the foolish thoughts out of her mind, constantly telling herself to stay calm and remain mature, she kneeled down to retrieve her belongings.

Grasping the folders within her hands, and neatly stacking them one on top of the other, a foot suddenly appeared from out of nowhere. Someone pressed their feet right below her face where she was kneeling, smashing Talent's fingers as she picked up her folders.

Quickly withdrawing her hand from underneath the culprit's shoe, Talent made an upward glance with a very malicious look in her eyes as anger took full control of her entire body. As she stood to her feet, she met the eyes of a much bigger and much meaner looking individual, with the same furrowed brow and that same angry glare, staring down upon her. Standing right beside her was a couple of her big, burly friends.

Instantly recognizing the angry faces as the exact same girls that constantly antagonized her in class the year before, Talent's anger began to boil even stronger.

She tried her best to remain calm about the situation, even showed some common courtesy. "Excuse me, you're stepping on my books," Talent exclaimed while constantly trying to extract her material from underneath the bully's foot.

But to no avail, it was no use.

Breathing erratically now, while doing everything within her power not to explode, Talent prayed. But all she seemed to hear was Grandma Clifton's words as they vividly kept popping into her mind. *Sometimes, you might have to beat the devil out of some folks in order for them to learn their lesson.*

And with that thought in mind, Talent decided right then and there to put an end to all their bullying ways, once and for all. She gripped her sharpened no. 2 pencil and deeply lodged it within the calf muscle of the main bully's leg. She quickly pulled it out and lodged it in her thigh, just to initiate the fight.

The bully's scream erupted from her mouth like the wellful cries of a fire truck. Loud and piercing.

As she doubled-over in pain, while constantly reaching for her leg, Talent caught her with a sharp upper-cut to the chin. She followed the upper-cut with a left hook to the jaw that sent her victim crashing to the ground with a loud thud.

"Boom!"

She lay their bald up in a fetal position, crying like a newborn baby as blood seeped from her wounds.

Talent's anger ran so deep within her that she contemplated stomping the girl while she was down, just to add more insult to her injuries. But she quickly decided against those actions due to the girls pitiful sobbing and the cries of agony that constantly escaped her mouth.

She surveyed the crowd, looking for the other two girls that were with her, but they had already left the vicinity. Realizing that they were nowhere to be found, Talent somewhat composed herself, picked her belongings up from the floor while keeping a very watchful eye on her surroundings, and calmly walked away.

Awestruck and full of fear, the students parted ways like the Red Sea as Talent maneuvered through the crowd, heading in her big cousin Liz's direction. By this time Liz stood there beaming proudly as she watched Talent make her way toward her.

Happiness couldn't begin to describe the feeling that Liz currently felt, after witnessing her little cousin defend herself. Or so it seemed.

Although she sat back watching the entire ordeal about to take place, she was determined not to get involved, which to a couple of her close friends seemed very odd. "Some things you just have to handle on your own," Liz told Shica and Sheena who were about to intervene on Talent's behalf when they realized she was about to be ganged. Instead, Liz stopped them, instructing them to wait.

Liz was glad that she stopped them. It allowed her to see just how far Talent would actually go in order to protect herself. She made her proud of how she handled the situation.

Finally making it to her cousin, Liz embraced Talent with a huge bear hug. "I bet they wasn't expecting that were they?" Liz whispered into Talent's ear before patting her on the back and seeing if she was okay. She knew that she was good, she just wanted Talent to confirm it for her. "Well, now that all of that is finally over with, come on champ before you actually make us late to class." Liz said in a humorous tone while releasing a tiny chuckle.

Upon hearing the word champ, Talent cringed. Regretting her current actions just that fast. She truthfully hated fighting with a passion and hadn't had to do so since defending herself against Liz a few years prior. She regretted that fight as well after realizing she hurt Liz pretty bad for trying to do the exact same thing, bully her.

Chapter 7

It was merely impossible for Talent to remain focused in class as the events from earlier that day constantly bombarded her mind. Knowing that at any given moment, Mrs. Nicole, or even worst, the police could come in and whisk her away, embarrassing her in front of the entire classroom.

She could see her teacher's mouth moving but had no earthly idea as to what it was that he was actually talking about. As she looked around the room to see if she was the only un-attentive person in class, she realized she was. With a goal of succeeding in school her lack of attentiveness made her feel bad. Talent prayed for God to give her the ability to concentrate, but the negativity from earlier wouldn't permit her to do so.

She really disliked the fact that Mr. Kerley, her new English teacher, was teaching and she was totally unable to learn whatever it was that was being taught. Especially since all of her other classmates seemed to be so enthralled with the lesson. So once again, she prayed!

Remembering a scripture that she had read earlier that morning, Talent asked God to take her troubling thoughts captive and replace them with thoughts of Him. She followed that request by quietly quoting one of the very first scriptures that she had ever memorized on her own. Matthew Chapter 11, verses 28 through 30.

Come to me, all you who labor and are heavy laden, and I will give you rest. Take my yoke upon you and learn from me, for I am gentle and lowly in heart, and you will find rest for your souls. For my yoke is easy and my burden is light...

She instantly felt better as soon as the last word of that scripture left her mouth.

She now truly understood why Grandma Clifton had always told her to pray whenever she felt discouraged or troubled about something. At first, Talent didn't understand because prayer never really worked for her in the past. But from that very moment, she decided to keep prayer a major part of her everyday life. No matter what.

Now fully energized and feeling as if a huge boulder had been lifted from her shoulders, Talent could finally focus on what it really was that she enjoyed doing most of all. Learning.

The anxiety and nervousness from earlier that day had completely subsided and she was more than eager to participate with the other students in her class.

Totally unaware of what the specific topic was, Talent knew for a fact that it wouldn't take her long to catch on. Especially since English had always been another one of her most favorite subjects.

She pondered over the petty incident yet again for another brief second or two. She wished that she had been the bigger person in the matter and chose a more mature approach in handling the situation altogether. But she refused to continuously ridicule herself about it any further.

As she turned her undivided attention back toward the skillful teachings of Mr. Kerley, whom at the time it seemed, was doing a fascinating job explaining how to properly write an essay on one of African American's most prolific authors, Mr. Richard Wright. Born in the soulful city of Memphis and also a Tennessee native himself, Mr. Wright wrote two of the most powerful books of his time called, "Native son" and "Black boy lost." Both books were inspired by certain unbelievable experiences from his Southern upbringing and also became best-sellers.

The more Talent listened to Mr. Kerley explain about the author's life, the more intrigued she became. She was extremely proud being a part of a race of people that was so determined to elevate themselves from America's bigotry and oppression "by any means necessary," as the late, great, Malcolm X would say.

She realized the continuous struggle that her people had consistently faced throughout history. From slavery, all the way up to current date. She then wondered, why would one race of people do all that they possibly could in order to deprive another one's race, the African American race, of the exact same opportunities that they had once been given to help advance themselves as well. Especially when they were all God's people.

What truthfully stemmed hatred, malice, and envy in people, anyways? And how is it that African

Americans solely became its main target for it? Talent silently asked herself as the all-so-inspiring words of dancer, poet, writer, playwright, civil rights activist, producer, and also director, the great Ms. Maya Angelou came to mind. *Still I rise,* she thought

"Still I rise," Talent quietly recited to herself yet again. Instantly recognizing the true importance of the words, along with its power, as she once again glanced around the classroom. *Especially, for the American Negro,* she thought. "And definitely for myself," she mumbled underneath her breath. She wondered who amongst her classmates, if any at all, felt the exact same way.

She relived the events from earlier once more, although she said she would not, embarrassed at how she allowed herself to become just as simple-minded and small as the people in which tried to bully her.

Talent thought that she had not ascended above the situation this time. She actually descended. But that was okay because she promised herself it would never happen again. She released the thoughts from her mind as far as she possibly could, once and for all.

She knew that the girl's behavior toward her had nothing to do with her personally but had to originate from their own personal battles with insecurities. And because of that, Talent never responded nor reacted to them at all, at least she hadn't before today, which in a sense, surprised even her.

So why was today any different than all the others, she questioned herself. And just as fast as the question had formulated itself into Talent's mind, so did the answer. *Because they really needed to be taught a valuable lesson*, the small voice stated.

Hoping that the altercation would finally humble the girls enough for them to turn from their wicked ways before they accidentally hurt somebody, or even worse, before someone seriously hurt one of them, Talent prayed for them all. She never wanted to see either of the occurrences ever come to past. *Life was far too precious to waste it all on such frivolity,* Talent thought as she cringed from picturing the catastrophic visions that could possibly be.

It was meant to be one of love, peace, joy, and happiness – not that of suffering, envy, turmoil, and strife, she admitted, knowing that all of the latter options led to sin and when sin fully matured, ended with death! Talent never wanted that for anyone. Not even for those who constantly made it their business to consistently persecute her day-in and day-out for the last couple years of her young life.

Life had already been far too difficult for her people. She would never be an addition to that struggle. This she knew. *I will be a solution for them someday*," Talent vowed. "A help and not a hindrance," she confidently spoke, as her own words brought a huge smile to her beautiful face.

Talent had dreams of molding minds like Mr. Kerley did with his teachings and like several other great teachers were doing at the time. Or had once done in their lifetime. Increasing the awareness and enlightenment of many so that they could honestly discern the lies that constantly restricted them from truthfully advancing in this all but equal, and very much separated world that we now have the privilege of finally calling home.

On that note, Talent began to vigorously participate in her classroom activities once again. The more Talent became involved with the curriculum, the quicker her day passed. And before she even realized it, her school day had finally come to an end.

She learned a multitude of different material that she couldn't wait to share with her little brother, Potential. And surprisingly enough, no one had confronted her about the incident from earlier. Well, no one from the principal's office had anyways, which was definitely a good thing.

A few other students, whom the girls had obviously been bullying as well, thanked Talent for standing up to the girls. They approached Talent as she neatly stood arranging her belongings on the top shelf of her locker as she was preparing to leave. Even shadowing her with small bits of praise. To them, it was a victory for them all.

Talent humbly accepted their gratitude, but quickly discarded their so-called acts of praise. Before closing her locker, she said to them, "Next time we'll continuously beat her down with love, instead of with our fist, knees, or pencils...ok?" Talent spoke those words while smiling at the young girls standing before her as she respectfully eased past them on the way to her bus.

They thought Talent was one of the coolest, hippest chic's in the world at that moment. All four girls smiled back in complete approval before replying, "Ok, you have yourself a deal Miss Talent Clifton." The young ladies watched as Talent's small frame disappeared around the corner of the hallway.

Finally making it to the front entrance of the building, Talent saw Liz waiting at the bottom of the steps so that they could share seats together on the bus ride home. Or so Talent thought.

Just as Talent was making her exit, Mrs. Nicole, along with two other professionally dressed men in dark suits appeared to her right.

"Excuse me, Talent!" Mrs. Nicole said with an extremely stern look plastered across her attractive face. "These gentlemen would like to ask you a few questions. Can you come with us please!" Her tone was very demanding.

Highly taken aback by her principal's cold demeanor and aggressive attitude, Talent never recognized the devious grin that was etched across her cousin's deceitful face.

"Now, let's see you get out of this one little Miss goodie two-shoes," Liz harshly stated to herself as she headed to board the bus alone laughing underneath her breath.

Chapter 8

Survivor was extremely proud of her children. Although she never deemed herself as a very religious person, she constantly thanked God for blessing her with two beautiful babies.

Up until the point of having her children, she had never known much about the true inner workings of God. But she definitely knew that he did exist. Survivor knew that God was responsible for the creation of mankind in its complete entirety, and that we were all made in his image.

Seeing that His creation was good, God had given man complete dominion over all His many other creations. Like the fish of the sea, the birds of the air and over every living thing that moves on the earth. Placing him just a little lower than His angels.

Survivor knew that God was a merciful and forgiving God. But most importantly, she knew that God so loved the world that he had given His only begotten son, (which is Jesus Christ) that whosoever believes in Him should not perish but have everlasting life. She knew all of this because of Grandma Clifton who constantly informed all of her children, all of her grandchildren, and even her great-grandchildren, about the greatness of God. She also constantly taught them about the death, burial, and resurrection of His son for as long as she could remember.

Survivor never understood much of it then as a child. But as an adult, and even more importantly now as a mother, she did. She was even more grateful that her grandmother had gladly taken the time out of her many arduous days to explain God's greatness to them every single chance she got. Which was frequently.

Survivor was also grateful because she knew she had done a lot of horrible things growing up in order to help put food in her and her siblings' stomach, and even worse things for clothes and shoes. Desperate times always called for desperate measures back in those days. Especially for African Americans, and especially for the uneducated, poverty-stricken, inner-city dwelling, American Negro child of the slums who were forced to grow up faster than your average kid. Every opportunity that presented themselves available to them needed to be seized whenever possible.

There was no such thing as modesty during those times because modesty led to starvation for those with no guts. And many died or had either become prey for the numerous other predators that compacted the extremely dangerous living quarters of Nashville's inner-city neighborhoods.

Although Big John and Mrs. B. Lee both worked full-time jobs at the time, it was still almost impossible for them to make a decent living for themselves on the wages in which they were paid back then. Especially with greedy landlords taking full advantage of most black families, overcharging them rent for housing spaces that were basically unlivable, or that probably should've been condemned.

The roof and floors of the house looked as if they were about to cave in on them at any given moment. And although they acknowledged this, the Clifton's still had no other choice in the matter but to call it home.

With so many extra mouths to feed, and not enough money for repairs, everyone in the Clifton household participated in renovating their home themselves. While the men were busy patching the leaking ceiling and laying sturdier pieces of plywood across the weak spots of the floor, most of the women were attending to the holes. They stuffed the holes with a poison-filled cloth that was laced with wire so that the rats couldn't chew through before covering it with wood themselves.

There was no such thing as not having a place to lay your head, or not having enough food to eat when it came to family, friends, and even certain strangers for the Clifton's. Even if they sometimes went without themselves, in which they actually did on more than several occasions. Especially Mrs. B. Lee.

Acknowledging this fact about their parents, Survivor and her brother Sam in turn did whatever they could or had to do in order to help out. Whether it be conning, stealing, robbing, lying, or cheating.

The two of them had committed many crimes breaking the law in several different ways, all in the name of family. But, from their point of view, their actions were definitely all justifiable, considering the circumstances.

A lot of responsibilities had been thrust upon the shoulders of Survivor and Sam. They had no other choice in the matter but to step up and step up they did! This made them both extremely quick-witted and definitely a lot keener. Especially when dealing with the everyday slickness of the hood.

Survivor, who was only fourteen years young at the time, was also responsible for watching her little brother Tee until one of her parents made it home from work. It was usually Mrs. B. Lee who made it home first. Big John never really made it in until late.

She had her little brother so much that the people in her neighborhood actually thought he was her child. Survivor allowed them to believe whatever it was that they wanted to believe about it. She observed the many disgruntled looks on the faces of their neighbor's and wanted to address them on several different occasions.

But she didn't.

Mostly because her mind was always overly consumed with whatever scam that they had planned for that day in order to feed themselves. It was never easy dragging their little brother along with them as they committed these capers. But their hands seem to always be tied. Having him with them made him a major accomplice to each of their schemes.

Looking back on it now, all Survivor could actually do was grimace. *What would've happened to him if we had ever gotten caught?* Survivor said to herself. She did all that she could possibly do to erase the troublesome thoughts from her mind, knowing very well that their parents definitely would've killed them both if they would have been caught.

Survivor sat in the quietness of their living room, rocking back and forth in her father's chair continuously pondering over all the ignorant things that she had done in her past. All the time, wondering to herself how she had actually made it through. Especially since so many others, who were definitely more fearless and far more intelligent or street savvy, had not.

And that's when it dawned on her as to who had been guiding and protecting her from all her disastrous ways for all of those many years. And that presence alone was God!

God allowed Survivor to come through so many arduous situations and near-death experiences for a reason. To prepare her for motherhood.

Motherhood is one of the most precious and greatest gifts that could ever be received by a woman during her lifetime. And Survivor now thrived in it.

Never realizing that she could love someone in the manner in which she loved her children, Survivor figured that this had to be the same exact way, if not extremely deeper, that God loved us.

So much so that He had allowed His only begotten son, Jesus Christ, to go to the cross and die for our sins in order for us to be saved. "Thank you, Lord Jesus!" Survivor earnestly spoke, while looking toward the ceiling as if she could actually see His face. "Ump... ump... ump," she genuinely gestured.

But before the feelings of happiness could soundly resonate within her and set the tone for the remainder of her day, in walked her niece Liz with a very distraught look plastered upon her face.

"What's wrong baby girl? Are you okay?" Survivor asked Liz with a voice full of concern.

Standing there as if in some type of traumatized state while constantly twirling her fingers, Liz never gave Survivor a response.

Survivor knew that something was bothering her niece, but she was unable to draw it out of her. She tried taking a different approach in the matter altogether. One in which she definitely hoped would work.

Easing toward Liz and placing a comforting hand upon her shoulder, Survivor calmly began to speak once again. "Come on baby girl, talk to me. Tell aunt Survivor what's troubling you," she said reassuringly. But still to her surprise, she received no answer.

Liz's eyes nervously darted all around the room from one corner to the next in complete avoidance of making eye contact. And what was once twirling fingers had now become extremely fidgeting hands. Furthermore letting Survivor know that something definitely wasn't right, sending all sorts of intense warning signs coursing throughout her slender frame.

Completely reacting off of her own mother's intuition, and almost on the verge of absolutely losing her cool, Survivor instantly grabbed Liz by the collar of her shirt, and with all seriousness began badgering her about her child who had yet failed to walk through the door of their home.

"Liz, where is Talent?" Survivor asked in an almost panic-stricken manner. "Is she in some type of trouble or something?" she continued. "Oh God! Please let my baby be okay, Lord, please!" Survivor begged. "Is she hurt, Liz! Huh? Is she! Is that the reason why you can't answer me! Tell me what's wrong with my child Liz. And tell me now!" Survivor demanded.

Liz had a very estranged look in her eyes as Survivor coldly stared at her in the most malevolent of ways. Feeling as if she had been repeatedly beaten all over her body by the continuous onslaught of her aunt's strong line of questioning, Liz wearily blurted out the answer. "The principal and two professional looking police dudes in dark suits held her after school okay! That's all I know!" Liz exclaimed exhaustingly before collapsing to the floor in a hysterical cry.

Upon receiving that information, Survivor was out the door with a quickness. She was heading directly to her daughter's school to find out what was going on with her child. She no longer heard the babbling words of her niece as she lay tightly balled up into a fetal position in the center of the living room floor. "I'm sorry auntie, I'm so sorry," she wept. "I promise I didn't mean for it to happen that way," Liz said, sobbing louder and louder with each and every word.

Chapter 9

Survivor weaved in and out of traffic like a crazed woman doing everything within her power to get to her daughter's school. She had a million different thoughts rushing in her mind all at the same time, causing her to press even harder on the accelerator of her father's huge sedan.

She blared the horn at the many other patrons that compacted the crowded streets in order for them to speed up, or to simply let her pass. But with no luck, and remaining at the exact same pace, it infuriated her even more.

Survivor's nerves were on edge. As her gut instinct kept telling her that Liz was somewhat responsible for whatever was going on with her child. She couldn't prove it as of yet, she thought, but she knew she eventually would. And whenever that time came, if it ever were to come, it was definitely going to be a serious problem! Survivor promised.

"That's why she had such a guilty look on her face when she first entered the house," Survivor said out loud to herself. She was gripping her father's steering wheel so tightly that the whites of her knuckles had begun to show, as she tried her best to control her anger.

Survivor knew that Liz could be a very vindictive person at times. But she never expected her to be that way towards her family. The thought of how she treated her family left her completely stunned. So much so that she had almost forgotten to make her turn.

She whipped the big sedan into the school's parking lot at the very last minute and Survivor pulled to a screeching halt.

She hit the steps, taking them two at a time, until she finally reached the main entrance where she encountered a janitor that was buffing the front lobby floor. "Excuse me, sir. Can you please direct me to the principal's office?" Survivor asked as calmly as she could possibly muster trying her best not to sound too anxious.

"Yes ma'am, just keep straight until you get to the end of this hallway and take a left. It'll be the first door on your right," the janitor said. After giving Survivor directions, he placed his headphones back into his ears and started bobbing his head to the beat, as he continued to work.

"Thank you!" Survivor yelled over her shoulder as she quickly darted off. But her words fell on deaf ears due to the loudness of the janitor's music.

Breathing a bit heavily now, Survivor entered the office only to find what looked to be the first janitor's co-worker cleaning its deserted space. "Excuse me, Miss, I'm here to see the principal. Is there any way that you could get her for me, please?" Survivor politely asked the woman wearing the Dunn's janitorial shirt.

Looking down at her wristwatch before glancing back into Survivor's doe-like eyes, the woman kindly notified her that everyone had already gone for the day.

"Gone for the day! What do you mean gone for the day!" Survivor aggressively screamed.

She obviously scared the mess out of the woman that stood before her holding the dust mop. "Ma'am, I'm just a janitor and I'm only doing my job," the woman timidly spoke. She tried her best not to ignite Survivor's anger any further than she already had.

"My child was held here after school today. Now you're standing here trying to tell me that everyone is gone! Naw, that can't be true!" Survivor yelled with a very deranged look in her eyes as she furiously stared the woman down.

Unable to accept the woman's answer as truth, Survivor dashed around the counter to search for her daughter herself, surprising the janitor lady even more.

"Hey! Wait a minute!" The woman shockingly voiced while back pedaling with her hands held out in front of her signifying that she didn't want any trouble just in case Survivor had come to attack her. Running herself into a wedged-in corner, with no other place to go, the desperate janitor lady began to speak once again. "Wait a minute! Listen, ok?" the woman voiced fearfully. She thought Survivor was coming directly toward her, which she was not. "There was a little girl here with the principal when we first arrived, along with two other men in suits that looked to be policemen! But they were leaving! I promise!" The woman exclaimed.

"Policemen!" Survivor yelled as she bolted from behind the counter of the office. She started running in the same direction in which she had come, straight out the double doors of the school, in what seemed to be only a few short steps. She jumped into her father's huge sedan once again and recklessly pulled away from the curb. She was driving even faster now than when she had first arrived.

Chapter 10

Recognizing that the coast was clear, and that she was now also at home alone, Liz finally pulled herself up off the floor and wiped away her so-called tears. She knew exactly how her aunt would react as soon as she revealed the news about Talent. But to her surprise, it worked out even better than she initially planned.

"Just like taking candy from a baby," Liz said with a devious grin as she giggled to herself. She started to perform a small celebration dance around the living room. "Let's see what they think of their sweet little Talent now," Liz stated evilly.

Liz took a huge bite of the sandwich that Survivor had obviously fixed for herself but left on the living room table before dashing out the door. "Dang, I'm good!" Liz confidently stated.

Dropping her book bag into the center of the floor, she headed out the front door in search of her two best friends, Shica and Sheena. These two friends were the girls who were going to help her so-called angelic little cousin Talent in the fight. She wanted to be sure to definitely give them a piece of her mind. *How could they be so disloyal?* Liz thought. *After all this time, how could they not know how I actually feel about her. Especially, when I've tried showing them on several different occasions,*" Liz said to herself. She became more and more upset with every step she took, as she strolled the neighborhood looking high and low for her friends.

Thinking back on the fight, Liz was actually devastated that the other two girls hadn't intervened on their friend's behalf and completely beaten Talent to a pulp. That was exactly what she wanted to see happen seeing as how the fight was her idea.

But as usual, somehow Liz's plan had obviously failed. Her so-called Miss Goodie two-shoes little cousin Talent had once again come out on top. *At least she had for the moment anyway,* Liz said to herself as she continued pondering over the scenes in her mind.

Making her way through the crowd, Liz watched Talent very closely as she drew near to her after the fight. Extremely disliking the fact that the other students had parted ways in order for her to do so.

"Look at this mess, they are moving out of her way like she's some type of royal princess or something," Liz remembered saying in disgust as Talent got closer and closer to her. She tried her best to conceal the hatred she felt in her heart for her little cousin. Liz plastered one of the fakest smiles on her face that she could possibly muster. One that had easily been detected by others as well.

Liz hugged her little cousin and whispered something into her ear that only Talent could hear as she still faked that same exact smile that she held moments ago. Liz assumed that no one else had acknowledged the disgusted look that she made behind Talent's back as they embraced.

But they had!

And those somebodies were Liz's so called best friends, Shica and Sheena, whom both were extremely shocked by their friend's reaction toward her family.

Chapter 11

Survivor had no idea what she should do, or in what direction she should actually go in order to begin the search of her child. She aimlessly cruised the blocks of her neighborhood back and forth in hopes of locating the vehicle that contained the two suspicious looking policemen. She hoped she was at least still accompanied by the professionally dressed African American female that just so happened to be Talent's new principal. But to no avail, she had no luck in spotting them anywhere.

An hour or so had passed since school had been released and still, up until that point, no one had yet to see Talent make it home. This caused Survivor to worry even more. "Lord! Please let my baby be okay!" Survivor begged.

Resting her head on her hands, she continuously gripped the steering wheel of the car as she engaged in prayer. Her nerves were a complete wreck at the moment. Survivor's beautiful face seemed to have aged several years from the increased stress of those tedious moments.

Tears flooded Survivor's eyes. But she refused to let them fall. Instead, she willed herself at that time to be stronger as she blinked away the watery substance that encompassed her eye sockets, until her vision had once again become clear.

"Get it together girl!" Survivor said angrily. She was upset at the fact that she had allowed herself to become so vulnerable because of her current situation. "What would momma do if it were her?" Survivor asked herself. She started remembering how Grandma Clifton had always told them to wholeheartedly lean on God during their times of trouble because he would definitely see them through it.

So lean she did.

She started giving God one of the most sincerely spoken prayers that she had ever prayed before in her entire life. And she meant every single word of it. But she was still unable to rationally gather her thoughts while continuously fighting the urge of having a serious breakdown. Survivor did one of the only other things that she had ever heard about doing.

She fully accepted Christ Jesus as her Lord and Savior, right there in the cramped confines of her father's huge sedan. Sitting on the side of the road of thirty-second and Clifton, parked just a few feet away from her home, she started to ask for help. "Help me Jesus! For I know that you're the only one that can truthfully do so at this time, and I promise to obediently serve you for the rest of my life!" Survivor vowed.

She stubbornly released a few tears that she tried so hard to keep within, but she could no longer do so. Survivor quickly wiped her face with the back of her hand smearing the tears until they were no longer visible. She checked her appearance in the rearview mirror to make sure that she looked okay.

And at that very instant, she heard a small distinctive voice whisper something softly into her ear. "Head home my child. But before you do, stop and put some gas in your father's car." The unfamiliar voice clearly said.

"Some gas!" Survivor surprisingly said.

She started looking around to see where the voice had actually come from. She did not locate any one to attach it too besides a drunken old man that lay slumped on the side of the wall several yards away. "Naw, it couldn't have been," Survivor stated to herself in unbelief as she gave the area another quick survey. She then checked the gas gage of her father's vehicle and realized that the little orange hand actually sat below the empty symbol by at least a quarter of an inch. Meaning that the car was strictly running off fumes.

"How long have I been driving around like this!" Survivor said obliviously. Instantly she pulled into Swett's gas station where the huge sedan suddenly sputtered to a complete stop.

She guided the huge car to a near-by gas pump with a push from a few good Samaritan's. Survivor exited the vehicle, paid the store attendant, and began pumping her gas. Before heading in the direction of her home, like the strange voice had suggested, for some odd reason she knew that heading home was the right thing to do.

She bided farewell to the men that helped her as she pulled out of the parking lot, waving goodbye to them as she made her turn. "Thank you, guys," Survivor loudly said appreciatively. Smiling for the first time since Liz had given her that oh so disturbing news about her child.

Survivor felt better now for some reason or another as she pulled into the driveway of her home, only a few minutes later. Survivor spotted an unfamiliar dark car sitting right in front of their house. One that contained three adults, and that of a young, teenage girl it seemed. "Talent!" Survivor hysterically yelled.

She leaped from the vehicle like an Olympics gold medalist running as fast as she could in order to get to her daughter with a very intense look of anger burning deeply within her eyes.

Survivor hurdled the bicycle that lay sprawled recklessly across the lawn of their home like a professional. And within another quick step or two she was snatching the car door of the stranger's vehicle open as she yelled obscenities at them as spit flew from her mouth like a ravenous dog.

"Momma!" Talent screamed embarrassingly, as Survivor pulled her from the backseat of the occupant's vehicle. She shielded Talent with her body while preparing herself to go into another fitful bout of her vicious rantings, but only to be stopped by the tranquil sounds of that very same voice from earlier.

"Remember your promise to me my child," the distinctive voice whispered tenderly.

Although it had been spoken to Survivor very softly, the impact of those words grabbed hold of her as if she was being aggressively apprehended by law enforcement. Instantly bringing a sudden sense of calmness to her once boisterous demeanor

"Forgive me Lord?" Survivor apologized.

As she looked up toward the sky, she pulled Talent into a tight embrace, hugging her as if she hadn't seen her in years. And that's exactly how it felt after being away from her daughter for so long without having a clue of where she was.

She's back now and that's all that matters, so thank you Lord! Survivor thought to herself.

Now, fully placing her undivided attention on the three authority figures that stood before her, she wondered, *how on earth am I going to get Talent out of this one?* As the wheels of her quick-witted mind speedily began to churn.

Chapter 12

Talent exited the schoolhouse with a smile as big as a crescent moon as she spotted her big cousin Liz standing at the bottom of the staircase. She never once recognized Mrs. Nicole and the other two strange gentlemen that stood to the right of her until they approached.

"Excuse me Talent, these gentlemen would like to have a few words with you. Could you come with me, please?" Mrs. Nicole said nonchalantly.

She then turned on her heels heading back inside the building with the two strange men following in close pursuit. She stood in the doorway looking towards Talent waiting for her to join them. Talent oddly looked at Liz, pleading with her eyes for her to come along. But strangely enough, instead of coming to her little cousin's aid, making sure that she was okay, Liz merely smirked and simply boarded the bus, shocking Talent in the profoundest of ways.

Talent watched Liz take her seat, never once making eye contact with her again as she stared straight ahead while speaking a few idle words to the individuals that was seated in front of her.

"Wow!" Talent solemnly expressed, extremely stunned by Liz's reaction toward her. She stood frozen for a brief second or two sucking in a few deep breaths of air in order to help relinquish some of her current frustrations. She stood still for a moment longer before following Mrs. Nicole and the other two strangers back inside the building where they waited for her as if she was some type of criminal.

Writing it off as fear on her cousin's behalf, Talent followed the trio to a near-by conference room that was adjacent to the principal's office. She sat in silence as the three adults discussed something majorly important just a short distance away. She was completely out of earshot, not able to hear a word that they spoke. Talent's nervousness was apparent. Her palms had become extremely sweaty as she continuously wiped them off on her pants. For the life of her, she could not stop fidgeting which made her feel even worse about the situation, whatever the situation was.

Never in a million years had she imagined her first day of middle school being like this. And possibly ending with her being escorted to juvie hall for simply defending herself. *But what else could I have done*, she thought.

Talent wanted so badly to cry at that moment, but she would not allow herself to do so. She had always been raised to know that tears truly served no purpose when faced with a crisis. Nothing but actions did. *And what better time than now for me to react.* She said to herself.

Talent inhaled a few deep breaths in order to help calm herself down. She quickly placed her game face on as Mrs. Nicole and the other two strange gentlemen joined her at the table with all of their information. This made Talent even more uncomfortable with the entire situation.

But yet and still, she remained poised knowing that it was in her best interest to do so at the time. Especially since her mother was not amongst them.

Talent witnessed on several occasions, watching numerous cop shows with her grandmother, just how supposed suspects constantly wedged themselves into an even deeper situation by opening their mouth. *And that was not going to be me*, she thought as she patiently waited for someone to tell her what was going on. She erectly sat in her seat, with her hands crossed in her lap, like the good little student she was.

Periodically they looked up from their documents long enough for them to make eye contact with Talent, then right back down at their papers. The two strangers never spoke a word. And neither did Mrs. Nicole who sat back observing the entire thing with a very watchful eye. Her behavior only irritated Talent even more.

She rolled her eyes toward the sky, obviously annoyed, while shaking her head out of pure frustration. She wondered how someone could speak so kindly to her during the earlier parts of the day, but have absolutely nothing to say now, or on her behalf to the police that were currently present. *What a fake!* Talent thought.

Finally, unable to hold in her silence any longer, she demanded one of the three adults that was currently holding her against her will to call her mother. "Look, if I'm in some type of trouble or something, then one of you need to be notifying my mother! Because I'm not liking this at all!" Talent said aggressively.

She stared at everyone in the room with her hands clinched into tight little fist as they rested on the tabletop of the huge conference room table. Visible for everyone to see.

"Trouble? Talent, you're not in any trouble darling." Mrs. Nicole stated speaking up for the very first time since they all entered the room. She sauntered towards her and draped her arm around the top of Talent's chair, giving a slight chuckle.

"Well, if I'm not in any trouble then, why are the police here?" Talent responded back sharply showing much more of her agitation than she had normally expected.

One of the strange gentlemen stood up from the table, ran his hands down his suit to smooth out the wrinkles, and readjusted his tie before he began to speak. "Honey, we're not policemen at all. Actually, we're recruiters from FCA - Flourine Cowan Academy. Have you ever heard of us?" he asked confidently giving Talent a brief second or two to respond.

"Y Y Y Yes, of course I have," Talent stuttered. She was now ashamed of her earlier behavior as she dropped her head into her hands, silently ridiculing herself.

Giggling at her reaction, the recruiter lifted Talent's head back upward as he continued smiling at her as they once again made eye contact. "Miss Clifton, or should I call you Talent?" the recruiter said jokingly as he continued on. "Our institution has been following you for a while now. Watching you excel academically, year after year. Which has been amazing. And we were wondering if someday, in the near future, if you might be interested in becoming a student at FCA. If so, then I definitely think that we can arrange for that to happen," he stated with a serious tone.

"Now, we're not the biggest of schools, but I can definitely guarantee you, that we're one of the most proficient and efficient schools around. Like that of Hume Fogg or a Montgomery Bell Academy, which are both great schools. But these schools and others have nothing in comparison when it comes to the solely black-owned establishment of Flourine Cowan Academy. FCA was founded in the wonderful year of God's nineteen hundred and nine on the small, segregated streets of Nashville, TN, and still stands to this very day," The recruiter proudly stated with his chest poked out and his head held high as his bright, beaming smile brought even more light to the highly radiated room, temporarily blinding Talent and Mrs. Nicole with its rays.

"F _ C!" the other recruiter loudly chanted, unable to restrain himself because of the love that he also felt for the barrier-breaking history that FCA, as an establishment, continuously upheld. His outburst tickled Talent and Mrs. Nicole both, tremendously.

"I'm definitely going to love this school!" Talent said, knowing that if it was up to her the decision would've already been made. But it wasn't. The choice solely belonged to her mother, which Talent prayed would definitely go in her favor. Attending a school as prestigious as FCA had been something that she dreamed about for years.

"So, what's up? Can we sign you up for the tour or what?" the recruiter who did most of the talking asked.

"Yeah, can we sign you up?" the other recruiter excitedly asked smiling from ear to ear as they both folded their arms across their chest. Both recruiters stood together leaning to the side. Then they stood back to back as if they were some type of posing rap group that had just completed their act.

Talent and Mrs. Nicole applauded the two men for their theatrics, laughing the entire time. Then the men took a bow before laughing themselves.

As bad as Talent wanted to say "yes" to the recruiters about the tour, she knew that she could not do so without the permission of her mother. In a gloomy way, she replied, "Mr. recruiters, Mrs. Nicole," Talent deeply sighed, "as much as I would truly love to say *yes* to this once in a lifetime type of opportunity on my behalf, I cannot. Because to do so would be a major injustice to my mother and grandparents. And I love them far too much to disrespect them, or to go against what I know is right. Even if it means never getting the chance to attend the school of my dreams. This is a matter that you'll have to take up with my mother, sir. As of yet, I'm not at liberty to be making those types of decisions for myself." She seriously stated.

Talent was hoping, in all honesty, that her mother agreed. Attending FCA was something that she had always wanted to do.

"Well, let's go see if we can get that permission then," one of the recruiters said smiling. And within seconds, they were all piled up in his dark-colored sedan heading straight towards Talent's home with the smooth voice of Ronald Isley crooning in the background singing about a voyage that he was taking to Atlantis…

Chapter 13

After all the commotion, Survivor stood there thinking of a way to free her child from the devastating grasp of America's penal system before it could sink its claws into her oh-so innocent flesh. Possibly ruining her life forever.

For many, many years, Survivor heard about, learned about, and actually witnessed firsthand, the catastrophic effects that inequality played in the lives of most African-American's. *This system is not about to get my baby. Especially if I could help it,* Survivor thought. She knew the promises that she had made to God about bringing Talent home safely. And she also knew that lying was prohibited. But God would just have to forgive her for the sins that she was about to commit because there was no way she was going to allow these two strangers to take her baby girl to jail. "Not today... Not tomorrow... Not ever!" she confessed.

Just as Survivor was about to go into her most cunning modes of deception, Mrs. Nicole and the two strange gentlemen introduced themselves. "Hello Ms. Clifton. I'm Mrs. Nicole, Talent's new principal, and these two fine men are recruiters from Flourine Cowan Academy. Better known to most as FCA, one of the most prestigious schools in the state. We are here because they are extremely interested in... well, maybe I should let them explain it to you," she said gleefully, stepping backwards as the taller of the two recruiters stepped forward and began to speak.

"Ms. Clifton, how are you? My name is E. L. Morrow, and as you've heard, I'm a representative of FCA. Now, on behalf of Flourine Cowan Academy...

"Hold on one second," Survivor chimed in. "Now, you did say recruiters, right?" Survivor said.

"Yes, ma'am," E. L. replied.

"So, you're not the police?" Survivor asked. "Because, if you are, and you don't tell me... Well, that's entrapment, you do know that, right?" Survivor said seriously as everyone present began to laugh. Even her.

"Ms. Clifton, I can definitely assure you that we're not the police," E. L. Morrow said snickering.

"Well, thank you Jesus! Because I sure didn't want to lie to y'all, but I would have if it meant getting my daughter out of a jam." Survivor said. "What! I would've," Survivor admitted as everyone continued snickering.

Mrs. Nicole and the other two gentlemen laughed even harder. They knew that Survivor was actually telling the truth. Everyone kidded around for a little while longer, laughing at one another's jokes and silly gestures.

Then the recruiter started to explain all of the details of the tour. Everything from the full-scholarship that Talent would be receiving due to her high GPA – all the way to the career-placement programs and the many other financial stability courses that had been implemented by the school.

After another brief session of serious questions and answers to make sure that she fully understood everything that was being said, Survivor set the date and shook all of their hands before departing.

Talent bounced around in pure excitement as she ran off to discuss the tour with the rest of the members in her family. Well, everyone except for Liz, because she was not there at the time.

Chapter 14

Liz dwelled in the shadows across the street from her family's home. She watched Talent as she conversed with a few more of their relatives, and a couple more of their schoolmates about something that obviously had her super excited. Her anger boiled deeply within her, and she was consumed with pure rage from the exiting taillights of the unmarked vehicle that was obviously leaving her little cousin Talent behind. She now realized that the latter part of her plan had failed as well.

But how? Liz thought to herself. *It should've been a one-way ticket straight to the juvenile detention center and out of my life for good.* She was furious at the excitement she was witnessing that should have been the complete opposite. "Dang! Dang! Dang!" Liz expressed angrily kicking over the neighbor's trash cans before slithering out of the yard like the venomous little snake that she was. Completely undetected.

Liz had written an anonymous note to Principal Nicole explaining in full-detail about the earlier altercation that had transpired between Talent and the so-called bully. But she completely switched their roles, making Talent the aggressor of the altercation and the so-called bully her weak and innocent little victim. Afterwards, she gave the letter to Shica and Sheena, her main two partners in crime, to secretly slide into Mrs. Nicole's private information box.

But little did Liz know, the bogus letter never made it to the principal. The two girls had flushed it down the toilet of the women's second floor restroom. Not only had Liz lost the letter, but she also lost the two closest people to her as well. Instead of helping her possibly destroy Talent's future, Shica and Sheena were now conjuring up a little plan of their own in order to give Liz a taste of her own medicine.

Later on that night...

Survivor could finally relax knowing that everything was finally back to normal as she laid in her bed contemplating over all the crazy events that had transpired that day. Never before in her entire life could she recall another moment being so hectic for her. Or one where she had been so remotely afraid. Except for the time when Potential, obviously unsatisfied with the rations that he had been given that day during lunch, decided to sneak a few extra pieces of meat for himself, without the acknowledgement of the adults, and was almost killed in the process of doing so. That day had to be the most-scariest day of Survivor's life now that she thought about it. And it probably forever would be.

"Ump!" Survivor grunted, as if she had taken a blow to the mid-section after recalling the horrible events of her past. She cringed deeply as if it had just happened to her all over again. Small sweat beads of perspiration magically started to appear on the front of her medium-size cranium.

As she blankly stared up at the ceiling for a moment, completely lost in thought. She once again thanked her heavenly Father for the much-needed protection that He had always provided for her and her family. She then snuggled her weary frame comfortably beneath the thick confines of her colorful blanket where she prepared herself for some much-needed sleep.

Survivor adjusted her pillow before closing her eyes, placing it in her favorite position as she shifted her body until finding that perfect spot within her bed. Then, just like that, she was out. Snoring just as loud as her father Big John, if not louder.

Chapter 15

The events of Potential's young life were many. And although he had only been living for such a short period of time, he had already faced death on more than a few occasions, surviving each and every incident only by the grace of God. Well at least that's what most believers in Christ Jesus would be quick to say anyway. And to be honest, they would be absolutely correct.

For those that knew Potential's earlier battles with death firsthand, also knew that it was merely impossible for him to pull through such devastating situations by his self alone. Especially at such a young age. God's favor was definitely upon Potential's life. And although He specifically placed it on the lives of all of His children, Potential's circumstances were much different by far. God was not a God of favoritism. Nor was He a God of partiality. But He did bestow His gifts upon us all. Through the overcoming of the many arduous episodes of Potential's young life, he would definitely fulfill his name - Potential.

Now, almost every parent has proclaimed that their child was blessed from birth, and some of the smallest things about their child would actually lead them to believing this. Something so simple as a smile from the child as the parent talked to them while making all sorts of strange faces and weird sounds, knowing that

84

the child couldn't possibly comprehend. But the parent's actions toward the child made that child react with a smile. This child's reaction would become the most miraculous event that they, the parents, had ever seen. Or so they would be quick to say.

But these reactions were not blessings at all. Well, at least not the miraculous ones that came from God. They were just "simple reactions." Something that most children did when entertained by some of those same exact gestures.

But Potential on the other hand was different to say the least. God must have definitely heard Survivor's prayer when she asked the Lord to send His angels to guard and protect her son in all of His ways, because he definitely did.

Potential's first bout with death was surely one that most kids wouldn't have survived. To be honest with you, a lot of adults had already lost their lives to it.

It all started with a so-called close friend of the family that Survivor and Mrs. B. Lee both entrusted to care for baby Potential while working the midnight shift at the local hospital. A job that they both recently landed at the time.

Now whoever would've suspected that the same hospital, in which they both now worked, that delivered Survivor's children, would also be responsible for saving her young son's life, just a few short years later. And of all things from alcohol poisoning.

Instead of giving Potential solid foods, such as mashed potatoes, vegetables, and fruit, the so-called friend of the family constantly pumped Potential's young body full of vodka in order to keep him asleep. Slowly destroying his barely developed organs more and more with each and every drink.

It all went unnoticed until one Saturday morning, as Mrs. B. Lee was babysitting her grandson, she wondered why he constantly kept crying and clutching at his stomach. Not thinking much of it at first, Mrs. B. Lee simply shrugged it off as nothing more than a mere stomachache. She knew that Potential was a growing child that could most definitely eat.

She gave him a small dose of castor oil, along with a cup of prune juice in hopes of making him use the restroom. She figured that this would definitely do the job, and before you knew it, he would be right back to normal once again, eating up everything in sight.

But that wasn't the case at all. As a matter of fact, the oil and prune juice only seemed to make matters worse for him. As soon as Potential engulfed the thick, funny looking substances, he doubled over, gripping his mid-section even more tightly screaming out in what appeared to be an extremely agonizing pain. He started spewing vomit all over the place. And his chest heaved up and down as if it was about to explode. It seemed like it was difficult for Potential to catch his breath as he constantly gasped for air. And his stomach performed this uncontrollable vibrating motion as if someone was punching him from within, totally distorting his handsome, young face.

Large beads of sweat broke out all over his small fragile frame. Everything that was happening to him scared the mess out of Mrs. B. Lee even more. Never in her entire life had she ever seen a body convulse so violently before. Especially one as small as her grandson's.

She seen everything from stab wounds to gunshots wounds, even the most stomach-churning aftereffects from untreated STD's. But none of that compared to what she was witnessing with her grandson

Mrs. B. Lee didn't have a weak stomach at all, none of the Clifton's did. She had even been responsible for dishing out more than her fair share of gruesome wounds herself, and none of them bothered her. She had seen so many wounds that it actually became normal for her to see. So normal that they literally gave her the moniker of the "Beer Bottle Queen" due to the fact that she had slashed, stabbed, sliced, and cut so many different individuals with broken beer bottles.

But this, this was different! Totally different! Mrs. B. Lee thought to herself.

Rushing over to the telephone, she quickly dialed 911 as fast as her stubby little fingers would allow. She then proceeded to frantically report every single detail of the events to the operator on the opposite end of the line as calmly as she possibly could. She constantly tried her best to utilize the breathing techniques that she recently learned during training.

After placing the call, Mrs. B. Lee waited for the ambulance to get there as she consoled her grandson as much as she possibly could. She wiped his body down from head to toe with a cool rag and showered him with multiple hugs and kisses.

Her nerves were a complete wreck. And from the looks of things, so was Potential who now looked to be completely dehydrated as his small fragile body quivered in her arms, making her more nervous with each passing moment.

Mrs. B. Lee impatiently paced the floor, constantly peering out the front door of her home, still cradling Potential in her arms. She felt as if she was about to lose her mind until she saw that the ambulance had finally arrived.

She burst from the house with a quickness as she frantically waved her arm from side to side trying to draw the attention of the paramedics. And before they could actually make a complete stop, Mrs. B. Lee was already halfway inside the back of the cab with Potential's limp body dangling from her arms. "Go! Go! My grandson is about to die!" she hysterically yelled as she beat on the side of the ambulance screaming orders as if she was an EMT worker herself.

Taking one look at Potential's limp, sweaty, little body, the real EMT worker instantly administered an IV into his arm in order to replenish his body with fluids when he noticed the apparent signs of dehydration.

When he safely secured his passengers, he gave his partner a quick succession of taps signaling her that it was now time to move as she rapidly skidded away from the curb.

They arrived at the hospital within minutes where the nurses speedily rushed Potential to a nearby examination room in order to run a few more test on him. After about an hour or so later, the doctor finally gave the results of alcohol poisoning.

"Alcohol poisoning! What the heck you mean alcohol poisoning Doc? Just what are you trying to say?" Mrs. B. Lee vehemently spoke with a very disgruntled look plastered upon her angry face.

The doctor patiently explained all of the specific details to her while expressing his concerns. He also notified her that children services had to be contacted, along with the local police, and that she would have to be detained until they arrived.

Upon hearing the doctor's statements, Mrs. B. Lee almost completely lost it. But she held her composure for the sake of her grandson.

Breathing deeply, she replied, "Okay, that's fine." She said with a tight mouth trying to hold back her anger.

Making her way to a nearby chair in the front of the waiting room, she anxiously waited for children services and the police as she steadily said to herself, "Lord, now don't you let these white folks start no mess up in here. Because if you do, it'll definitely be on!" She took her seat, crossing her legs like the dignified black woman that she truly was, and she waited.

Chapter 16

The time had finally come. Children services diligently bombarded Mrs. B. Lee and Survivor both with a multitude of questions while the two police officers stood close by taking notes, trying their best to catch them in a few lies.

They played the game of bad cop, good cop, asking the same exact questions while twisting them in a variety of ways in hopes of confusing them. But none of it worked.

Even if they were guilty, they would have never fallen for that trick anyhow. They both knew that each of them had already faced the interrogation scenario on more than several occasions in the past and had always come out unscathed.

They patiently endured the very intense line of questioning with ease. And after two long grueling hours of constantly being badgered, they were finally released.

After retrieving their stories in full detail, and acknowledging that they were actually telling the truth, the officers finally issued a slew of warrants for the so-called friend's arrest. Mrs. B. Lee and Survivor both made a few solemn promises of their own right there in the presence of the cops.

"Officers, we truly appreciate you doing your job. But you know that those warrants will be of no use if it just so happens that we're the ones to find her first, right?" Mrs. B. Lee seriously stated as she stared both officers directly in the face.

From the look in her eyes, they could definitely tell that she was serious. "Now ma'am, we're going to act as if we didn't just hear that," the more serious officer responded. They shook everyone's hand and gave them a business card as they quietly exited the room, mumbling to themselves the entire way.

Following those events, Survivor and Mrs. B. Lee camped out down the street from the woman's home daily, for hours at a time, determined to give her exactly what she deserved. And they had no plans on stopping until they finally met with her face to face.

Several days passed, and still the women had no luck in locating her. The two women finally decided to allow their so-called friend to trap herself, knowing that eventually she would.

Snakes could only hide for so long, Mrs. B. Lee told herself knowing that it would only be a matter of time before she slithered from her dark, little hole. *And whenever she does, I'll be patiently waiting*, Mrs. B. Lee promised.

Easing hesitantly away from their spot of seclusion, they were still hoping to see her, which never happened.

Chapter 17

After several months passing, Potential was finally back to his normal little, jovial self. And so were most of the Clifton family. The Clifton's, along with all of Mrs. B. Lee's sister's, were preparing themselves for their extravagant, fun-filled, family weekend. This was an event that consisted of plenty of food, plenty of laughter, plenty of dancing, a lot of loud music, several different card games and much, much more! They were so eager that it seemed as if the festivities had already begun.

Mrs. B. Lee, Lil Bay, Lil Sugar and Helen all went shopping to gather the remaining items for the night and kindly paid the cashier. Rose was already outside screaming at the top of her lungs. And laughing amongst themselves, the sister's figured that her and Big John, were once again acting a fool with one another because that was something that they always liked to do. Especially when they were drunk, so they paid the noise no mind. At least until it dawned on them that neither of them had been drinking at the time.

Rose, who was actually the smallest sister in size physically, was definitely the feistiest of them all verbally. She kept the sisters in combat regularly whether it be with others or each other.

As they got closer, all they could hear was Rose screaming. "Winch! We're about to carve our names all over yo' body with these straight razors as soon as we get our hands on you! And you can believe that, like you believe in Christ Jesus, you low-down heifer!" Rose continued.

Unaware of who it was that was about to be beaten down, the ex so-called friend of the family searched the premises, waiting to see the altercation, having no earthly idea that she was the actual target. Not until she finally made eye-contact with her old friend, Mrs. B. Lee, along with all of her sister's.

The angry scowls that masked their faces let her know exactly who they were talking to as panic struck her body like a blow from a sledge-hammer. She was completely frozen in her tracks like a deer staring into oncoming headlights. And once she finally regained her composure, it was entirely too late.

Those short, few seconds was all the time that the sister's needed in order to grasp several different parts of her robust frame and devour her like the pack of wild lioness that they actually were.

Well, everyone except for Rose, who really wasn't a fighter at all. But she was definitely one of the greatest commentators that the hood had ever seen. She bounced around from foot to foot, throwing jab after jab, constantly giving the crowd an outstanding play by play of the fight.

"Ooooooohh! Lil Bay slams her to the ground by her hair. As Helen rapidly rains down a beautiful combination of punches to the head, neck, and torso area, in lightning-fast successions," Rose announced holding her hand as if she was actually speaking into a microphone for real. "Feet fly, as Sug sends kick after kick to the woman's mid-section," Rose continued while constantly performing her shadow-boxing exhibition for the crowd.

"Oh snap! Was that a knee to the face!" she excitedly screamed covering her own face with her hands as if she could actually feel the blow herself. "Oooo, that was cruel! Is that even legal?" Rose asked the individual standing close to her pushing her hand towards his face as if she was still holding a mic. The onlooker simply shook his head and laughed. Not knowing exactly how to respond. Rose ran through the crowd slapping hi-fives. She was truly putting on a show for the spectators who were now mostly watching and laughing at her instead of the fight.

When the smoke cleared, and the fight finally came to an end, Rose paraded around even more poking her chest out as if she had actually thrown down with them herself.

Noticing Rose's antics, although still very much driven by their adrenaline, all the sisters could do was laugh. "Girl, get in the car fool!" Helen said as the sisters were shaking their heads at Rose's humor, knowing that even when she was serious, she just couldn't help it.

Rose was famous for constantly assuring folks that she had some sister's that would rip them apart if they were to ever put their hands on her during arguments, and low and behold she did. Just as they were departing, she was proudly telling everyone present about how tough her sisters were. The lesson had been delivered with multiple punches, kicks, and jabs, leaving scars that the woman would never forget. Physical scars just as well as mental.

But the mental scars that the woman would carry is what satisfied Mrs. B. Lee the most. Although it might not have been the best way of resolving things between them, she could sleep peacefully now knowing that the woman who was responsible for almost taking the life of her grandson, would never forget the price that she paid for her actions.

And like Grandma Clifton once used to say, "Sometimes you might have to beat the devil out of folks in order to teach them a lesson." And on that note, Mrs. B. Lee started humming an old Negro spiritual...

Chapter 18

Potential's second bout with death, was actually one of his own doing. And although it was an extremely serious ordeal at the time, later on it became one of the funniest episodes that the Clifton family had ever experienced, even to this very day.

It was a Saturday afternoon, and the house had finally cleared out from the card game the night before. Survivor decided to cook a quick meal for the remaining members of her family along with the few close friends that still occupied space in the Clifton home as well.

Draping on her robe, Survivor headed to the kitchen where she searched through the refrigerator trying to decide what it was she wanted to eat.

She had a taste for breakfast food. As her eyes landed on the carton of eggs that sat closer to the front, she knew that the eggs wouldn't agree with the substances she had recently consumed just a few hours earlier. So she decided against it.

Rummaging through the refrigerator at least two more times sliding packages to and from, Survivor was still indecisive. She stood there with the door ajar for several more minutes gazing at the contents as if something new would magically appear. But it didn't. Feeling a small twinge of irritation building up inside of her, she finally closed the door and headed straight toward the kitchen cabinets.

She figured if she could decide on what she wanted the sides to be then choosing a meat to complete the meal would be nothing at all. And she was absolutely correct.

After extracting the four cans of creamed corn from the cabinet, Survivor decided to peel herself a few potatoes, dicing up some onions as well in order to give it a little more flavor.

Afterwards, she seasoned her flour because she knew that whatever meat she decided on would definitely be fried. And within seconds, she came up with the idea of pork chops to compliment her meal perfectly. On top of that, the grease would truly help settle her stomach like it always had on the many other occasions before. Her mouth started to water in remembrance of the meat's taste.

An hour had passed, and Survivor had finally finished cooking. She started making plates for everyone before eagerly preparing her own. She said Grace and then they all tore into their food as if they were starving.

After feeding their faces, the adults sat around laughing and joking from the many different incidents that had transpired the night before. Each of them doing their own personal re-enactment of whom they thought were the funniest. Which was most definitely between Big John and Aunt Rose because they both were hilarious. Especially once they got a little "Buck Juice" in their system, as Uncle Sammy's wife, Vis-zal, would so famously call it, making reference to liquor.

Now Val was another very funny individual belonging to the Clifton family as well. She was running neck and neck with Big John and Aunt Rose herself on being among the funniest. And when they were all three together, they were known for completely turning the party out! And the adults loved it. But so did Potential who was always somewhere sitting close by listening, especially when there were no other kids around.

Using some of the material that he had heard from the adults, Potential would sometimes create his own games. Entertaining himself. This allowed him to use a part of his brain that most kids did not as he constantly bounced around the house getting into all types of mischief.

At times, he would even get a few of the adults to participate as well. Especially when he was playing the role of a comedian and mimicking Richard Pryor.

Potential would get so caught up in character at times that he would even curse. And although this had gotten him popped on more than several different occasions, the adults couldn't do anything but laugh. And so did he.

It truthfully surprised them that someone as young as Potential could recite Richard's act so fluently. But what they didn't know was that when Big John and Mrs. B. Lee wasn't around, Potential would sneak into their bedroom and listen to it, learning the complete album word for word.

Richard Pryor wasn't the only comedian he would listen to either. He also knew the entire act of Ma Mabley and Redd Foxx, placing him at the top of his class in curse words 101.

Potential knew that he could possibly get into trouble for this. "But I have to do it," is what he would tell himself. As he was reciting the last of Richard's words about Mud bone and getting closer and closer to the end of the joke, Potential started inching further and further out of the living room toward the front door, constantly checking his surroundings. When he noticed that the coast was clear, he let off a vicious barrage of curse words before dashing out of the room, completely missing the first few steps and almost bursting his butt.

The adults looked at one another and fell out with laughter as Survivor screamed his name. "Potential!" She shook her head from side to side in shock before releasing a small chuckle of her own. "Lil' bad Rascal," she said jokingly as Potential smiled to himself.

He then went outside and started searching the yard for a big enough rock to throw at the neighbors' dog. "If I get a beating for that one it'll be worth it because that was a good one. But who knows, if I stay out here long enough she might even forget about it." Potential said, chunking his first rock.

"Aaaarrkk!" The dog yelped causing Potential to smile even harder.

Chapter 19

The feeling Potential received from striking the dog with a rock was a good one. A very good one. But his initial reaction from it was the best, so he thought. It definitely sparked a fire in him to drive the dog completely insane, causing the dog to do everything within its power to reach Potential. He was only denied by the shortness of his chain, which Potential took advantage of.

"Maybe next time, you big mutt," Potential said to the dog as he constantly prodded at him with the stick that he held in his hand. The dog fiercely snarled at him through the fence. He knew that the dog had to be wishing he could one day sink his teeth into him instead of always gnawing on the metal that stood between them.

Finally acknowledging his defeat, the dog trotted away towards his water bowl where he took several huge gulps before lying down under the tree, steadily eyeing Potential the whole entire time.

Realizing that more than an hour had passed by, Potential assumed that he could finally make it back into the house unscathed. With the adults laughing as hard as they had been earlier, he figured that he should definitely be okay. *After all, it was only done in fun,* he thought. But still to play it safe, Potential decided to use the back door.

Once around back, he peered inside to make sure that everything was copacetic. Discovering that it was, Potential slowly began to make his entrance. Pulling open the screen door, it made a loud screeching noise. Potential shushed it as if he was actually talking to another human being. "Ssshhhhh!"

He waited a few more seconds before actually going inside. Then he stood in the middle of the kitchen floor listening to his family who seemed to be still enjoying themselves He even found himself laughing at a few of their jokes, instantly covering his mouth to stifle the sounds of laughter. He actually found their jokes to be quite funny.

"Lord, it must be meant for me to get a whooping today or something. I swear it seems like everything I do is trying to get me in trouble! From the scary sounding screen door to my big mouth!" Potential stated.

He playfully quoted a prayer that he would always use on his mother to get him out of a beating. "Now Lord, you know that my skin is light, and that my body is too frail to possibly be a match for the rough, rugged cowhide of my mother's belt. So please make her arms too heavy to lift and her hands too stiff to grip, so that I can possibly avoid this butt whooping that I'm about to get. Amen!" Potential said giggling.

He reminded himself to put a little cooking grease on the hinges of the door to stop the squeaking. He overheard his grandmother telling someone once before that you could use a little cooking oil on everything, and it'll shine like new.

He had even witnessed her greasing Big John up with it once or twice when he had been too exhausted to do it himself. Before lying him on their plastic covered couch, she was mumbling something under her breath about not having her sheets smelling like a "dang-on fish-fry." Or was it chicken?

Either way, if it was good enough to put a shine on his grandfather, Potential thought it definitely had to be good enough for the hinges of that old screen door. He instantly started scanning the kitchen for the big, blue Crisco can full of grease that normally sat somewhere close to the stove so he could carry out his plan. He quickly realized that the can was nowhere in sight.

But what he did find sent his stomach rumbling and growling like that of an angry lion. His eyes became fixated on the huge stack of pork chops that sat in the center of the stove.

Suddenly, all the playing that he had done earlier now made him hungry all over again. So, he decided to help himself to another piece of meat while no one else was around. He soon realized that the only thing that was preventing him from having it was his height. At the time, Potential was not tall enough to reach the top of the stove.

He searched his surroundings for a chair to find none available. He assumed the adults must've had them all in the living room. So Potential settled for the next big thing. The huge pots and pans that were kept underneath the sink.

Moving silently, Potential opened the cabinet. He found the perfect size pot, one that Mrs. B. Lee and Survivor both used when cooking greens. But there was one problem. The pot was tightly wedged in between two other pots of the same size and getting it out would definitely make too much noise, causing him to be detected. And he wasn't trying to get caught.

All he wanted to do was eat and go into his room to take a nap without being noticed. But it didn't seem to be working out that way.

As Potential stood in front of the stove, scratching his head, the most brilliant idea crossed his mind, or so he thought.

"Hey, why don't you just let down the oven door and climb up that way?" Potential told himself in all foolishness. He knew that it wasn't really a good idea, but he pulled the door open anyways and hoisted his little chunky self upon it.

Wobbling harshly, Potential still paid the stove no mind due to the fact he was so engrossed with accomplishing his goal. He was almost there. "If I can just get my fingers on the edge of the plate I could actually slide it to me," Potential told himself.

As soon as he was up on his tip-toes, stretching his arm out as far as he could, it flipped!

"Ba-ba-ba boom!"

The stove was now trapping Potential's poor little scrawny frame underneath all of its weight and he let out a piercing scream.

Hearing the noise, the adults instantly jumped to their feet and rushed toward the kitchen. And what they witnessed upon arriving actually traumatized them all.

The stove was completely toppled over, food was thrown all over the place, and the only part of Potential's body that could actually be seen was his leg.

"My baby!" Survivor hysterically screamed quickly darting towards him. But Mrs. B. Lee was already there. Tossing the stove back into an upright position pulling Potential free.

Now cuffed in her arms, Mrs. B. Lee burst from the backdoor, running full speed toward the hospital, which was only a couple blocks away, with Survivor right on her tail screaming frantically at the top of her lungs. Blood drenched Mrs. B. Lee's shirt as her and Survivor reached the front desk of the emergency room demanding to see a doctor.

"Lady we need a doctor!" They both screamed in unison.

Looking up, the charge nurse instantly went into action. She quickly picked up the phone, spoke a few words into the receiver, then speedily rushed around the counter to check Potential's vital signs, before rushing him away only a few seconds later.

Within an hour or so, the main doctor sent for Survivor and Mrs. B. Lee. He notified them both that the only damage Potential suffered was six stiches to the inside of his lower lip, which was amazing due to what happened. He also had a large knot on his head that would eventually go away.

There were no broken bones. No concussion. No head trauma of any kind. And no internal bleeding. Only a few abrasions here and there that would easily heal with time. Both women once again thanked God for protecting their child before showing that same gratitude toward the doctor who kindly accepted with a smile.

Before walking away, being a very spiritual man himself, the doctor shared a few words of his own. "God is a merciful God. One that truly protects his own. There's no way possible for a child that size to come away from an accident like that, with only six stitches to the mouth unless the Lord was involved. So, make sure that you keep him on the right path. God is definitely about to do some incredible things in this young man's life."

Survivor's mind instantly diverted back to something the McCreary's had told her shortly after Potential was born. *Your son has the potential of becoming a very great man in this lifetime. But it solely depends on the decisions that he will make for himself as he constantly matures.*

And from that very moment, Survivor knew that she had to find the spiritually blind couple called the McCreary's so that she could inquire about this so-called right path that everyone kept speaking about. Especially since it involved her son.

Chapter 20

The McCreary's...

Many years had passed by for the McCreary's. And after a numerous amount of surgeries, today would be the day that they received their sight. And this day was one of the greatest days of their lives, outside of giving birth to their child.

Today they would finally have the opportunity of seeing God's wonderful creation from their very own perspective. They would no longer be viewing the world by ear alone anymore. Nor having their daughter, Dorothy, describe the sceneries of their beautiful surroundings to them ever again. The only thing that stood between them seeing through their own eyes were the remaining bandages that still covered their eyes. But they would shortly be removed.

Several different emotions traveled through the McCreary's mind. Emotions that still could not be controlled no matter how hard they tried. Although they spent several hours in prayer beforehand, nothing at all seemed to prepare them for this moment.

It's true that their nerves were on edge, but the one thing that the McCreary's were not was worried. They knew that their Heavenly Father had already blessed them both when they gained their eyesight through the miraculous hands of Dr. Wiseman.

He was an incredible ophthalmologist. They knew he would probably never receive the proper recognition that he truly deserved by his Caucasian colleagues and counter-parts, only because of the color of his skin.

Dr. Wiseman was undeniably one of the greatest minds to ever enter the professional field of medical science. It was because of that, that the McCreary's had chosen him to perform each of their eye surgeries. He also successfully completed the job well under the number of surgeries that other physicians declared it would take in order to get them to the point where they currently stood today. But with no guarantee's or assurances of course.

But Dr. Wiseman on the other hand, did give those guarantee's which he solely based off of hundreds of hours of scientific research that he diligently performed on the human eye for the last several years. And at any given moment, he would be able to fulfill his promise. And the McCreary's knew it.

So, as they sat in the quaint little office, making small talk with their daughter, while steadily trying to caress one another's nervousness away by rubbing one another's hand, in walks an athletically built, caramel complected, African American male with a warm, radiant smile.

His long white lab coat looked to be tailor-made-to-fit, as it perfectly draped every inch of his muscular physique. He held within his left hand an odd-looking clipboard. "Ladies, gentlemen, sorry to have kept you waiting so long. But a doctor from another floor needed my assistance with a few things, so I decided to lend him a helping hand. I hope you don't mind." Dr. Wiseman sincerely said as he closely examined all of the details from his post-operative sheet, making sure everything looked exactly how it was supposed to be after their last surgery.

"Oh, not a problem at all, Dr. Wiseman. As a matter of fact, we needed a little extra time anyways so that we could help get our nerves together." T. Thomas politely stated as they all sat upright in their seats eagerly awaiting the news.

Just as it was one of the greatest days of the McCreary's lives', it was also one of the greatest days of Dr. Wiseman's life as well. God was using him as an instrument to perform the miracle of giving the blind sight. And for that, he was truly grateful.

That moment was completely priceless for Dr. Wiseman. Up until that point, nothing had been more special. As he slowly began removing the bandages from the McCreary's eyes, he silently prayed thanking God for the opportunity.

He gently extracted the last few pieces of gauze, then disposing his gloves before washing his trembling hands. Dr. Wiseman performed a quick double-check on all fifteen parts of the McCreary's eye socket. Observing everything from the optic nerve to the vitreous humor, in search of any type of hairline scaring or tissue damage of any kind. He found nothing at all, which was definitely a great sign.

And without further ado, he placed two flimsy pair of dark shades upon their eyes to help with any type of sensitivity they could have due to any brightness. Then he prepared himself for the outcome. Taking a few deep breaths as his heart beat rapidly within his chest, Dr. Wiseman finally asked the McCreary's to open their eyes. For a moment nothing happened. "Mr. and Mrs. McCreary, will you please attempt to open your eyes for me?" Dr. Wiseman once again requested.

He slightly felt a twinge of nervousness as he still received no response from them, and the room grew eerily quiet when all of a sudden, a loud piercing scream erupted from inside the room sending a reverberating echo traveling all throughout the empty hallways.

Rushing to her mother's side to see what was wrong with her, frightened by her sudden outburst, Dorothy began to panic.

Dr. Wiseman instantly grabbed all the proper utensils he would need in order to run some more test.

But as he sprang into action, getting everything prepared, Mrs. Ida B began to speak. "Oh my God! Everything is even more beautiful than I had ever expected it to be," she said in a low, soft whisper. Crying uncontrollably, she now stood in the middle of Dr. Wiseman's office gazing at all the contents that decorated the walls. Steadily she started thanking her Lord and Savior, Jesus Christ.

T. Thomas consoled his wife, pulling her into his strong arms and rubbing her back before kissing her tear-stained cheeks. "Are you okay honey?" he softly asked into his wife's ear as he continued to hold her.

Looking up into her husband's handsome face for the very first time, Mrs. Ida B. McCreary passionately kissed him. "I am now, darling. I am now," she said.

Dr. Wiseman and Dorothy both sat back admiring the couple enjoy their very first moments of sight together before quietly closing the door behind them as they entered the hallway to give them some privacy.

Chapter 21

Glancing at her wristwatch, noticing that she and Dr. Wiseman had been conversing for almost twenty minutes, Dorothy suggested that they head back inside to check on her parents.

"Time travels quickly when you're enjoying yourself, doesn't it?" she stated, totally oblivious to the time as well.

Dr. Wiseman simply agreed as he opened the door of his office and stepping to the side so that Dorothy could enter through. "Indeed, it does, my dear. Indeed, it does," he replied with a smile.

Dorothy eased passed him, making sure not to brush up against him, all the while thinking to herself, *what a fascinating person he is*, before, actually thanking him for his courteousness. "Thank you, Dr. Wiseman," she politely said entering the room. As she entered the room, she laid eyes on her parents, who were still embracing one another in the center of the floor as if they had been dancing. Seeing that moment shared between her parents completely stole her heart.

They didn't acknowledge Dorothy, as of yet. And for her, that was absolutely okay because she fully understood that this was their moment and not her own.

Plus, her mind was still somewhat consumed with the conversation between her and Dr. Wiseman.

Dr. Wiseman had discussed some very interesting things with Dorothy. Things that she never would've believed if she hadn't heard it from him personally. Like the fact that he had grown up not too far from the hospital, in a housing development called Preston Taylor Homes. A place where poverty ruled. A place where murder, robbery, drug dealing, drug use and prostitution was just a normal way of life for them. All the things that hindered a person from getting ahead, she thought.

But Dr. Wiseman had made it through, and he was proud of his upbringing. "Because it made me who I am today," he stated. After continuously explaining about all the love and support that the people in the 'so-called ghetto,' actually shared amongst themselves, Dorothy understood.

Dorothy had once heard a saying that said, "It takes a village to raise a child." After hearing Dr. Wisemans story, along with watching him conduct himself in a professional environment, she knew that the housing development called "Preston Taylor Homes," had to be one heck of a place in order to raise the man that stood before her.

Dorothy thanked God for His magnificence as she eased alongside her father, sliding her hand off into his, gripping it tightly. And for the very first time in their lives, the McCreary's finally got the opportunity to see their child.

They thought she was the most beautiful thing that they ever would see. A perfect mixture of them both. Dorothy was tall, toned and athletically built like her father. With a slenderness that truly complimented her femininity. And the same long, healthy, auburn-reddish colored mane as her mother.

But her eyes are what captivated them most of all. They were the lightest, prettiest green that one could ever imagine. Clearer than the most expensive of emerald. Hypnotizing you with just one glance. Giving her the appearance of a human Barbie doll.

Placing her hands upon Dorothy's face, in order to feel the smoothness of her flawless skin, Mrs. Ida B. stared in complete awe. She wondered if by any chance, if she looked the same way as tears instantly fell from her eyes. "Darling, you are so beautiful," Mrs. Ida B told her child. Trying her best to control her tears, but it was impossible.

"So are you mother, so are you," Dorothy sobbed in return.

T. Thomas pulled his two favorite women into a tight embrace so that they all could share a group hug. "Thank you, Lord!" T. Thomas said, squeezing his girls even tighter before planting a kiss on their cheeks, shedding a few tears of his own.

The moment at hand was priceless. One that neither of them would ever forget. Dr. Wiseman allowed the family to enjoy it without saying a word as he wiped away a few cascading tears himself. He knew that it was unprofessional of him, but he couldn't help it. His spirit had been touched in such a profound way.

God had once again made the impossible – possible, Dr. Wiseman said silently as he gathered himself to read the post-operative procedures to the McCreary's for a second time to make sure that they fully understood.

After finishing the reading, Dr. Wiseman then opened up the floor for questioning. Just in case anyone had some concerns about anything. But none of them did. He scheduled the McCreary's an appointment for the following week before walking them to the door.

They mingled with small talk for another brief second or two, then shook hands. "Well, I guess this is it, huh?" T. Thomas asked. Adjusting his glasses as he grabbed his wife's hand.

"I guess so. Are you ready?" Dr. Wiseman replied, patting T. Thomas on the back with a smile.

"Dr. Wiseman, we were born ready. Isn't that right honey?" T. Thomas asked his wife, who simply responded with a smile as she led him out the door.

As Dr. Wiseman watched the McCreary's walk down the long, shiny hallway alongside their daughter, Dorothy, all he could do was smile himself. "God is so amazing!" he expressed.

Closing the door to his office as a young African-American woman, wearing a nursing scrub replied, "That He is Doc, that He is!"

And that woman was Survivor Clifton.

Chapter 22

The elevator reached the first floor quicker than usual it seemed as Survivor made her exit with a smile. She spoke to those that were present as she passed by. And they kindly returned her gesture.

Realizing just how beautiful the day was, Survivor chose against dining in the cafeteria and decided to walk to the corner store on 18th and Jefferson to snatch her a turkey on rye. A sandwich that she had grown to love.

It was only a few blocks from the hospital, and she thought the walk would definitely do her some good. Plus, she needed the exercise. Survivor hadn't worked out in over a month. Which for her was unusual. That was something that she had regularly done before getting the job. She was still in phenomenal shape. But she knew that in order to maintain her physique, she would continuously have to keep working out. Especially, now that she was getting older.

Too many of her friends had already gotten bigger, either from having kids or just simply over-eating. But Survivor wasn't having it. She knew that her body was God's temple. A possession that he had given her to cherish. So, she would treat it as such.

And with this newfound motivation, she changed directions. She headed straight toward the main entrance where she would have to climb a slightly steep hill in order to begin her journey.

Rounding the corner of the hospital's first floor to make her exit, Survivor passed the popularly known African-American doctor named Dr. Wiseman who was making a remark of some kind about "How amazing God was," while staring in the direction of an older Caucasian couple and what looked to be their caregiver. Although unknowing of all the facts, Survivor still found herself replying.

"That He is doc, that He is!" Survivor said as she continued moving toward her destination without a second look.

Pushing her way through the double doors, Survivor's mood took a turn for the worse as an instant sense of dread suddenly consumed her body, shifting her attitude from joyful to skeptical in the blink of an eye as if she was in some type of danger.

Survivor scanned her surroundings, looking for something out of the ordinary and came up with nothing. But her senses were telling her otherwise as the hairs on the nape of her neck stood at attention, triggering something deep within Survivor's spirit. Everything looked as it always had, she thought, or so it seemed anyways.

There were no ambulances pulling into the emergency entrance, frantically hauling someone inside of the hospital with screaming doctor's shouting directions to the nurses. And the security guards were still at their normal post flirting with every single female that passed their booth.

Nor were there any type of individuals frequenting the emergency room doors as it normally was. Little kids with cuts, bumps and bruises and adults with a lot of the same, but only more severe. Or the panic-stricken teenaged mother's, who had no earthly idea as to what to do with their children's agonizing cries. All was quiet.

Survivor felt empathy in her heart for the young girls, and even wanted to cry with them at times. She vividly remembered the many difficult and frustrating days of being a child while constantly trying to raise one. Especially if you were stuck raising that child alone like she had been.

By mistaken identity, Talent's father had been hauled off to prison where he would spend the rest of his life, for a crime he didn't commit. And although evidence clearly proved that he was innocent, the judge still sentenced him to life behind bars without the possibility of parole. More so for the color of his skin, opposed to him actually committing the crime, which shattered Survivor's heart into a million pieces.

If it wasn't for her mother, Mrs. B Lee, there's no telling what the final outcome would've been for the life of her and her child. Because, through her mother, God had provided the appropriate strength for Survivor to carry on. And by God's grace, and His grace alone, so would they. She closed her eyes to help block out some of the images that linked her to the pains of her past before, silently saying a prayer.

Chapter 23

Re-opening her eyes after the completion of her prayer, Survivor found herself face to face with a very attractive Caucasian woman around her age.

"What in the world!" Survivor expressed surprisingly as she stumbled backwards a little, placing her hand over her heart in shock. "Oh my goodness, you scared me," Survivor said. Finally looking up into the woman's face after catching her breath.

"Ma'am, I am so sorry! I promise I didn't mean to startle you. I recognized you standing here in tears, and I wanted to make sure you were okay. You are okay, aren't you?" The woman genuinely asked in a very concerned tone as she observed the familiarity of Survivor's face. But she couldn't quite put a finger on how she actually knew her.

"Yes ma'am, I am fine. But thanks for your concern though. And thank you for checking on me as well," Survivor appreciatively replied. She was still doing her best to conceal her true inner feelings on the matter at hand but was unable to do so. And before she knew it, she was rambling, something that Survivor had never done, especially amongst strangers.

Feeling as if she had already expressed a little too much, Survivor turned in an attempt to leave. But the comfort of the strange woman's spirit wouldn't permit her to do so, causing Survivor to continuously carry on in conversation.

She started to explain in full detail the similarities between herself and the young teenage mothers. But she still spoke with much skepticism. "Not too long ago, that was me over there," Survivor said pointing toward the four teenage girls with the flustered faces as they cuddled and rocked their children in an attempt to keep them from crying. But they were failing miserably. "And at times, it really bothers me to see my people struggling so bad. Especially when the so-called powers that be refuse to get involved." Survivor frustratingly stated.

"Powers that be? What do you mean?" the strange woman asked.

"The government!" Survivor exclaimed rashly. "But you wouldn't understand," she continued, feeling a bit irritated and agitated all at the same time. The exact same way she felt when she first exited the hospital doors moments earlier.

"Of course I would," the stranger replied. "You're talking about oppression, prejudice, and racism, right? I understand those things whole-heartedly. Although I'm Caucasian, my parents and I received ridicule and discrimination to its highest degree, especially for choosing Meharry Hospital over the so-called prestigious white hospital throughout the city of Nashville. Once the public got a whiff that the lead ophthalmologist was actually African American, we really caught it then. Death threats and everything. But, you wouldn't know anything about that, would you?" The strange woman asked. "So, trust me when I tell you my parents and I definitely understand the vileness of man. Especially the so-called God fearing, white Christian ones." The strange woman added. As she disgustedly shook her head. "Like God would actually make one race of people superior over another. Foolishness!" The strange woman said with a fire in her tone before respectfully introducing herself.

Survivor stood there in silence completely flabbergasted by the woman's words. Her mouth flew open in true amazement.

"By the way, I'm Dorothy. Dorothy McCreary. And you are?" Dorothy said extending her hand for Survivor to shake.

Shock appeared all across Survivor's face. And although she was trying her hardest to respond, she couldn't seem to formulate the words, leaving Dorothy's hand hanging in mid-air.

"Ma'am, are you sure that you're okay?" Dorothy genuinely asked once again before allowing her hand to fall back towards her side. She was completely dumbfounded by Survivor's reaction.

Finally regaining her composure, Survivor sincerely apologize, "Dorothy, I am sooo sorry! But I promise you I was not trying to be rude. It's just that, well, we've actually met before."

Dorothy's concerned face quickly became one of masked confusion. While staring into Survivor's eyes, she was trying to decipher if she was actually telling the truth. "What do you mean, we've already met before?" Dorothy asked.

Unsure of where she should actually begin, Survivor excitedly started to just speak. "Well, several years ago at this very hospital, you and your family approached me about my son. As a matter of fact!" She said as she started to closely observe her current surroundings. "In this exact same spot!" she added.

Once again surveying the patient pick-up area that she had frequented several years prior, Dorothy's mouth hung agape in shock unable to believe her ears.

"My name is..." Survivor started saying, but before she could possibly complete her sentence, Dorothy already blurted out her name.

"Survivor! Your name is Survivor!" she excitedly screamed grabbing Survivor up in an unexpected bear hug, rocking with her profusely as she continued to speak. "And your son's name is Potential, right?" Dorothy rhetorically asked stating the obvious more-so than asking a question, tightly embracing Survivor once again.

"Those eyes, I knew it was something extremely special about your eyes. But I just couldn't put a finger on it," Survivor said expressing even more gratitude with Dorothy when the thoughts of what was actually happening to her finally registered. "Dorothy, when I tell you that my entire day has been a blessing for me, I truthfully mean it! But I never expected God to do this!" Survivor said in a praising manner as tears of joy affectionately poured from her doe-like eyes.

And upon making reference to God, along with using the word "blessing" all in the same sentence, Dorothy instantly took Survivor's hand, quickly whisking her away towards the hospital's courtyard where her parents quietly sat watching the immaculate scenery of perfectly manicured flowerbeds, beautifully aligned maple trees, and their very first descending sunset together, hand in hand. Reminding you of something that should only be captured in a love scene of a movie.

Chapter 24

"How could a scenery as beautiful as this possibly be described. Especially one that was so breath-takingly radiant," Mrs. McCreary said as T. Thomas gently slid his wife closer to him on the seat that they shared together, making the moment even more romantic for them.

They admired the magnificence of God as they stared off into the horizon, watching the reddish-orange hue of the sky change into an assorted variety of deeper blue's, softer pink's and lighter purple's. The beautiful colors gave the appearance of something that could only be imagined in a storybook or fairytale.

At that specific moment, the McCreary's made a vow with one another to never miss another sunset for as long as they lived. Mrs. Ida B. snuggled in closer to her husband's body, placing a comforting hand on his chiseled chest. Although the body consisted of and also performed several different unique and extraordinary functions, for them, sight was definitely one of the greatest gifts that God ever bestowed upon man. And now that they had finally received their sight, the McCreary's had every intention of truly enjoying it.

As they continuously basked in the glorious beauty of their current surroundings, the McCreary's instinctively allowed themselves to once again view the world from the perspective in which they had for so many years; closing their eyes and attentively listening to the sounds of nature.

They were able to pick up every distinctive sound, like the cracking of acorns by a hungry squirrel, or the sporadic flapping of a hawk's wings as it hovered above in search of prey. They also heard the small pitter-patter of children as they ran in the distance. Having no idea that the children in which they both heard were actually Dorothy and Survivor coming to greet them.

As the two women entered the courtyard, Survivor's nervousness increased by the second. And so did Dorothy's excitement. She couldn't wait to reunite her parents with this very special woman from their past and vice versa.

For several years the McCreary's had been concerned about Survivor, yearning to know that she and Potential were okay. And in less than a minute they were all about to receive their answer. Survivor held a lot of those same sentimental concerns about the McCreary's as well.

Survivor searched for the McCreary's for many years after their encounter with one another, but she continuously came up empty handed. She even pulled up their old hospital records, but still nothing appeared. She finally came to the conclusion that the McCreary's were no more than guardian angels who were sent to deliver God's message concerning her child. And since that day, she had never forgotten it.

Survivor started replaying Mrs. Ida B. McCreary's powerful words over again in her mind as they approached them from behind.

And sensing the closeness of his daughter's presence, T. Thomas was the first to acknowledge their only child. "Hello, my darling, your mother and I were just beginning to worry about you. We were thinking that maybe you had forgotten all about us and run off to live happily ever after with that extremely handsome and very intelligent ophthalmologist that we noticed you fondly observing earlier," T. Thomas said teasingly, trying his hardest to conceal the smirk that currently covered his face as he continuously stared up at the sky.

"Oh dad, now that's just absurd! Would you stop it, please!" Dorothy replied, embarrassed by his statement while casting her head in a downward motion, blushing and quickly fanning him off. She didn't think that her father had witnessed her eyeing Dr. Wiseman. But truth of the matter, she had been.

Dorothy's cheeks were as red as beets as her beautiful smile fully extended itself from one ear to the other, making her even prettier than what she had naturally been before. And Survivor, who only stood a few steps behind her, was the first to notice. Quickly leaning towards Dorothy, whispering into her left ear. "Aaaawwww! Ain't that cute," Survivor said chuckling lightly.

Dorothy playfully swatted her away before resuming the conservation with her parents. "Now how on earth could I possibly run off and forget my two favorite people in the world and expect to live happily ever after," Dorothy said to her parents. "But, I do have a surprise for you though," she continued, fidgeting with anticipation as she finally made her way around the swing to be face to face with her parents, leaving Survivor behind in order to conceal the surprise. "Mom... Dad..." Dorothy hesitantly began as if she were carefully gathering her words as she constantly twirled her fingers, which was something she had often done as a child, when she was nervous. "As I said before, I have some interesting news to share with you. News that I most definitely know that you're going to love..."

But before Dorothy could get to the major details of the story, T. Thomas politely intervened. "Excuse me darling, not to be rude or anything, but if you're about to disclose this incredibly great news to us now, shouldn't we at least ask Survivor if she would like to join us. You see, that way we can all receive it together," T. Thomas surprisingly stated nodding his head with a huge smile, thinking *not only do I know it all, but I also see it all... Even those things that are far behind me.* He started smiling even harder watching his daughter's astonished response as she stood there completely frozen.

"What's the matter, my dear? You look as if you've just seen a ghost. Or should I say, heard one." Mrs. Ida B. McCreary humorously stated as she spoke up for the very first time since her daughter's arrival as she continuously stifled her laughter, and repeatedly patted her husband's knee as if to say, "good job."

The looks that were plastered upon Dorothy and Survivor's face were priceless. Indescribable even. They constantly questioned themselves in their perturbed, young minds, wondering how her parents could've possibly known about the surprise.

There's no way that they could've saw me. Survivor thought, still thinking that the McCreary's were blind. She confusingly shook her head. *Nor could they have heard me either. Because I never actually moved until Dorothy began speaking. Which even then was only slightly,* Survivor still stated to herself, still in disbelief, as she looked over at Dorothy, who seemed just as perplexed and still very much highly disoriented from her father's statement.

Dorothy stood there completely dumbfounded, watching her parents with a very blank and unreadable stare, trying to decipher what was actually going on. She knew that her parents received visions from time to time about a lot of things, but she never knew they had visions about anything as simple as this.

Dorothy had no earthly idea as to how important it truly was for the McCreary's to once again be reunited with Survivor and her young son, Potential. There was definitely about to be trouble and the McCreary's needed to try their best to divert it if they could.

Because what was about to happen, if their vision served them correctly, would possibly put them all in harm's way. Everyone including Dorothy. And that wasn't a price the McCreary's were willing to pay.

Chapter 25

Realizing that the cat was completely out of the bag, and that their surprise had become a complete bust, Survivor finally made her way from behind the swing. Where she battled with a slew of many different emotions. She was both nervous, but still very much excited. Fearful and partially anxious, but also very confident as well. When it actually came to meeting the McCreary's once again, after such a long period of time, each and every last one of these emotions showed in Survivor's body language as she approached them.

This reunion had been a long awaited one for them all. The McCreary's greeted Survivor with nothing but open arms and a face full of joyful tears as they embraced her one at a time with Mrs. Ida B. McCreary taking the lead.

The two women hugged as if they had missed one another for years. And believe me, they had.
T. Thomas proudly beamed from the sidelines, patiently awaiting his opportunity to do the same. Which presented itself available to him before the completion of his final thought. Gingerly moving in Survivor's direction, T. Thomas tenderly placed his hands on the outside of her shoulder blades where he slightly held her with outstretched arms in order to take in the fullness of Survivor's beauty as the darkness of her smooth skin

shined like a star in the night. "I can see that life has definitely treated you very well over the years, my dear. Honestly, you haven't aged a bit," T. Thomas sincerely expressed as he caressed Survivor's face with the back of his hand before placing a light peck onto her right cheek. Then pulling her into his warm embrace for a hug of his own.

Sensing that there was no better time than the present, Survivor attempted to pose her question. But before she could do so, T. Thomas had once again intervened.

"Ssshhhh... just know that I know. Okay? Even about the many questions that you're currently wanting to ask." T. Thomas said with a slight chuckle as he released Survivor from his caring embrace so that he could finally explain, hoping that she would fully understand.

He motioned for the girls to sit and occupy the swing that he and his wife shared as he stood. T. Thomas moderately began the conversation, closely observing to make sure that he held their undivided attention. "God has always shown me that we would cross one another's paths again. But he never showed me when, where, or how exactly it would happen, until today." T. Thomas admitted while looking directly into Survivor's eyes before continuing. "This morning, after my prayer, but while I was still meditating, an angel of the Lord appeared to me in a vision. Showing me today's events exactly as they would occur. Everything from receiving our eyesight all the way up until the point of you and Dorothy's arrival," he said.

"From the receiving of our eyesight," Survivor silently repeated as she unconsciously stood from the swing. She was doing her best to comprehend what had just been said. But couldn't. "Hold up! Wait a minute! Are you actually standing here trying to tell me that you guys can see now, Mr. McCreary?" Survivor voiced out loud with much emphasis, obviously taken aback.

She confusingly shook her head as if she was trying to rid her brain of T. Thomas's words. Survivor looked at him and then to Mrs. Ida B. McCreary in an oscillating type of motion for some kind of confirmation but received nothing.

Completely at her wits end with the entire ordeal, she tossed both hands into the air in utter defeat. "You know what, I don't think that I can take much more of this... I'm done!" Survivor said somewhat brokenly. She was trying her best not to drop her head. But it was almost impossible for her not to do so, especially after encountering so many different things all at once.

Recognizing Survivor's distress, T. Thomas gently caressed her hand in hopes of settling her down. "Let me finish my dear and afterwards, I promise that you will understand," T. Thomas reassuringly stated, smiling his most genuine smile at Survivor which instantly relaxed her sudden sense of anxiety. His touched caused her to feel as if she had just been sedated as she once again took her seat. "Are you sure that you're okay?" T. Thomas asked, looking at Survivor with genuine concern as he continuously caressed her hand.

Assuring him that she was, Survivor politely asked that he continue. She was hoping she did not ruin her chances of hearing the rest of what T. Thomas had to say about his vision. "I promise you, I am fine, Mr. McCreary. Please, carry on," Survivor respectfully replied.

And gazing even deeper into Survivor's eyes while searching her face for any signs of uneasiness, he found nothing that concerned him and once again began sharing his vision. "As I was saying, before being so rudely interrupted," he continued, smiling at Survivor as he still held on to her hand. "...an angel of the Lord appeared to me in a vision this morning. Showing me every single event in its complete entirety, from beginning to end. Everything from the receiving of our eyesight, all the way to you and Dorothy entering the courtyard together in hopes of surprising us. And as difficult as it was for me to do, I had to conceal it from each and every last one of you. Even my wife who I couldn't tell until the time appropriately presented itself," T. Thomas stated. "Which is exactly what I was doing when you guys approached us from behind."

He gently started to pat Survivor's hand once more before finally releasing it. After filling them all in on a few other minor details about his vision, T. Thomas grew eerily quiet. And as if in some type of coma-like trance, he accurately began quoting the angel's request in its exact words, taking on a voice that they had never before heard, leaving everyone speechless while watching in true amazement.

"For thus says the Lord," T. Thomas began. "Go to the middle swing that sits directly in the center of the courtyard and anoint that spot with the special oil that you keep contained in the alabaster flask. And do this without the detection of your wife or any other patron that may be frequenting the area," said the angel of the Lord. "Because, if by any chance this solemn act of sacredness is revealed or exposed to anyone, other than yourself, not only will my curse be placed upon you, but it will also be placed upon your family as well. Once again stripping you of your eyesight, but also taking away your keen sense of sound, leaving you with only three of your natural five senses, along with your rational ability to think so that you can continuously ponder on the disobedience that you have displayed towards the Lord your God." T. Thomas specifically quoted before continuing.

"But when, and if, you are to carry out the things in which I've asked of you correctly, then my blessings you shall receive. And receive more abundantly. Exceedingly, multiplying you and making your descendants as plentiful as the sands of the earth. Never to be removed. Just as I did my faithful servant, Abraham. Supplying you with knowledge, wisdom and true understanding to its highest degree. One that far exceeds the value of all earthly wealth combined." He added.

T. Thomas continued on wrapping up his message with one last and final statement. "Silver and gold will be a useless commodity for you. For happy is he who finds wisdom and he who gains understanding. Because his proceeds are far better than the profits of silver and his gains better than fine gold." T. Thomas concluded.

And as if suddenly coming out of his coma-like trance, he exhaustingly leaned on the swing sets railing trying desperately to catch his breath. Extremely thirsty and also fully fatigued, he slowly dabbed away the few droplets of sweat that formulated on the brink of his brow, and completely unaware of what was actually going on with him at the time, T. Thomas opened his mouth yet again for a third time saying, "Remain completely still, without making a sound until the sky above becomes a multitude of many different shades and the sun appears to be a reddish-orange color in hue, showing only a third of itself to the world! And these things I have done as well," T. Thomas confidently stated as he constantly started repeating the day's date over and over again for no apparent reason. Which just so happened to be June eighteenth. The same exact day that Mrs. Ida B. McCreary shared her vision with Survivor about her son several years prior.

Finally taking notice of the day's date for the first time herself, Survivor finally realized it as well. "Oh my God! Today is actually the day we met, isn't it?" Survivor surprisingly asked in true amazement partially covering her face with her hands. As her sudden look of amazement now turned into a complete mask of fear in what seemed to be a mere manner of seconds.

"Indeed it is my dear, indeed it is," T. Thomas reassuringly expressed as he stared directly into Survivor's doe-like eyes. He watched her beautiful brown face scrunch up into several different abnormal expressions from her instant surprise. And knowing that Survivor couldn't possibly withstand much more, T. Thomas did all he could to help simplify the remaining parts of his vision without losing the potency of its message. As he delicately explained the most intricate details of what the angel of the Lord showed him with much subtlety.

Humbly lowering his tone of voice to an almost soothing whisper, he continued on, still maintaining eye-contact. "Everything was exactly as it had been before as you sat there in the patient pick-up area of the hospital cradling your son, while waiting for your father to pull the car around so that you could finally go home," T. Thomas told Survivor as he patiently began replaying to her the ending of his vision. "But this time, as Dorothy led my wife and I past you on our way into the hospital, from out of nowhere a little boy appeared. He was around the same age that Potential would probably be now, I'm assuming. But he never spoke a word. He simply sat there studying us as we approached you." T. Thomas further explained.

"And the closer we got, the more the little boy eased forward as well. Still, never speaking a word though, but instead he was listening intensely. As we once again went through all of the old details of our first meeting together until Big John finally uncovered the face of what we expected to be baby Potential, but it wasn't." T. Thomas stated.

"In the place of what should've been your sons handsome face, was only an empty black hole. One that released these extremely loud and manic screams, like those from an emergency vehicle penetrating the air with this unbearable noise that drowned out everything surrounding it except for the crying sobs of the little boy, who was now repeatedly begging for your help, even referring to you as his mother as if he was actually your son." T. Thomas concluded wiping the newfound sweat from his glistening forehead. Before lowering himself onto the ground in order to take a seat himself.

Upon receiving this information, Survivor instantly began hearing the wailing cries of sirens somewhere far off in the distance. Sounds that seemed to be drawing closer and closer, followed by the faint sound of Potential's weak and exasperated voice constantly calling out to her for help.

"Momma, help! Help me momma, please! I need you! They're hurting me momma, hurting me badly!" Survivor heard her son say as clear as day in her mind as she broke into a full-fledged sprint towards the hospital's main entrance, where an influx of emergency vehicles of all types had recently pulled to a screeching halt from every direction.

Bouncing from vehicle to vehicle like a crazed person in search of her son, Survivor could still hear Potential's voice as it constantly reverberated in her ear. "Potential, I'm coming baby. Mommy's coming ok. Just hold on!" Survivor commanded screaming into the sea of strange faces that currently surrounded her on every side as she frantically ran from one vehicle to the next, continuing the search for her son, but still unable to locate him.

Recognizing Survivor's apparent distress, a couple of law enforcement officers along with several other EMT workers tried their best to assist her. But the incoherence of Survivor's current state-of mind wouldn't allow her to comprehend any of it.

She had built a mental blockage within her that only allowed her to see and hear the face and voice of her son which only seemed to add even more chaos to her already fragile situation.

Profusely sweating and feeling as if she was about to vomit at any given moment while standing in the midst of the crowded area, Survivor once again heard the whimpering whispers of a small voice coming from somewhere close behind her. And initially thinking that it was one of the McCreary's, she instantly turned on her heels in the brink of tears only to find no one there. "Am I losing my mind?" Survivor questioned herself scanning the area in search of the McCreary's once again. Hoping that she was wrong, but quickly realized that she wasn't.

Then all of a sudden, just as it had happened before, that same exact voice whispered its request to her once again. "Survivor, check the time before it's too late," the strange voice demanded.

So, looking down at her wristwatch for the very first time since she had actually taken her lunch break.

Survivor recognized that the current time was the exact same time that it had been when she gave birth to Potential several years ago. "What the...!" Survivor shockingly expressed. As her knees buckled from underneath her and her body hit the hard, concrete pavement with a loud thud. "Boomp!"

And now, Survivor lay sprawled out in the exact same spot where it had all begun. From the meeting of the McCreary's to the reuniting with Dorothy, and now this. All she could honestly think about before fully succumbing to the darkness that so patiently awaited her on the other side was the dream that Grandma Clifton had recently shared with her days prior. Which, was very much almost identical to that of T. Thomas McCreary's vision...

And, with this final thought in mind, Survivor was out! Speedily drifting towards the cold, deep, darkness and beyond.

Chapter 26

"What happened?" Survivor groggily asked trying desperately to lift herself from the ground thinking that she was still outside. She had no earthly idea that she had been admitted into the hospital as a patient due to her extremely high blood pressure level.

All Survivor remembered was the strange whispering voice in her ear that was constantly asking her to check the time. After the voice, all she remembered was everything going black. Even though all this happened hours ago, she didn't remember much more than that.

The stress and strain of the latter part of Survivor's day had obviously taken its toll on her, causing her to faint. She was still a bit delirious when nurse Vickie entered the room explaining in full detail Survivor's current predicament in a way that only a professional could. But Survivor fully understood firsthand what she was explaining to her.

How could a day that began so perfectly possibly end up with me being peeled from the pavement outside of the hospital in which I work? And admitted as a patient, surrounded by a slew of very unfamiliar faces. Survivor thought.

Faces that she all deemed as foreign due to the constant blurriness of her still recovering eyesight. She was totally unaware that the people in the room was actually her family. Everyone was in full attendance supporting what they all hoped would be a very speedy recovery on Survivor's behalf as they crammed inside the small hospital room. Completely over capacitating the visitor's quota by at least a half dozen people.

Even her good friend Tina was there, whom probably shouldn't have been the first face that Survivor had seen once she actually come to, but it was. And, seeing her face first, took Survivor by surprise in a very huge way.

"Oh my goodness! What the what!" Survivor startlingly yelled. She leaned as far away from the individual as she possibly could without falling from the bed in order to help fully adjust her vision where she could get a better look at them.

When she finally realized that it was Tina, Survivor playfully took a swing at her. "Girl, you scared the mess out of me, what's wrong with you! What you trying to do, kill me! With yo' boo-ti-ful self," Survivor said laughing. Syllabifying the word boo-ti-ful with emphasis on each sound in order to drive home her point.

Somewhat slightly offended by her good friend's statement, Tina quickly countered back with a jab of her own. "Oh, no you didn't Lil' Ms. Stop, drop and hit the concrete as hard as you most possibly can! I know you ain't talking," Tina sarcastically replied casually placing the palms of her huge hands onto her widely indented hips as she mockingly rolled her eyes.

The two women stared one another down as if they were about to come to blows. Survivor sat as tall as her weak frame would allow, preparing herself for whatever was about to come. Because she had never been the type to back down from anyone and regardless of what her current predicament might have been at the moment, she wasn't about to start today. Sick or not, Survivor would most definitely fight. That's just who she was.

The atmosphere shifted from peace to pandemonium in the blink of an eye with Tina standing in the center of the floor clinching and un-clinching her huge fist, glaring menacingly into the eyes of her so-called good friend as Survivor challengingly matched her stare. The behavior of these two women was absolutely baffling, surprising the others in a very profound way. Leaving, everyone questioning whether or not they were actually really friends to begin with.

The McCreary's finally stepped forward trying to nullify the situation between them by bringing some type of civility back into the equation. And once that occurred, Survivor and Tina both erupted with laughter.

"Aaahhh, we got you! We can't believe you guys actually fell for that!" Survivor said.

"Man, you suck!" Both women screamed in unison slapping hi-five while laughing at the sullen looks that was now plastered across everyone's faces as they continuously vowed to repay them.

And with a shared laughter amongst everyone present, Tina gleefully hugged Survivor's neck.

"Ouch...ouch...ouch! Wait a minute – hold up!" Survivor painfully groaned looking at Tina with a painful expression as Tina quickly released her.

Tina jumped backwards checking on her friend, patiently awaiting Survivor's response so that she would know what to do next. "What's wrong? What is it? Did I hurt you?" Tina nervously asked.

The others looked on in genuine concern while Survivor steadily sat there grimacing.

"Uuhhmm...uuhhmm nothing. I just needed for you to get your big behind up off of me before you begin to squeeze too hard like you always do. I don't even think you recognize your own strength. Like that time on Easter Sunday when you accidentally dislocated three of Pastor London's fingers from a simple handshake. As a matter of fact, you're the reason why he just started giving everybody in the congregation the "fist bump" after church anyways. Now, what person in their right mind just want some dap after a good sermon, huh?" Survivor mischievously stated.

The entire room erupted with laughter, even nurse Vickie, who was running the last of her test on Survivor so that she could be discharged. And feeling a bit unprofessional due to her sudden outburst, nurse Vickie solemnly apologized. "Look you guys, I'm so sorry for laughing but that was hilarious. I just could not help myself," nurse Vickie said with another small chuckle. She notified the family that everything was finally back to normal and that Survivor was free to go. "Get on out of here with your crazy self. And for future references, leave people alone, okay?" nurse Vickie jokingly stated constantly shaking her head from side to side with a huge smile etched across her face as she casually made her exit from the room.

And, upon hearing the good news that Survivor was okay several of her family members had done the same. Everyone except for Talent and Potential, of course, who patiently waited for their mother to get dressed. When she was dressed Survivor and her children all departed the building together hand in hand. She had one of her children on each side of her, both extremely elated to be in their mother's presence again as they strolled.

Chapter 27

Once outside, the McCreary's stood close to the exit along with the rest of Survivor's family. They finally got the opportunity to formally meet Survivor's children who had tremendously grown over the years. Especially Potential who looked identical to the little boy that T. Thomas had seen in his vision, but he decided to save that conversation for a later date.

Survivor had already been through enough for one day and he wasn't about to add to it with his newfound discovery. T. Thomas thought as he eased alongside his wife, who was now introducing herself to the kids, smiling broadly as she shook their hands. "Hi, I'm Ida, Mrs. Ida B. McCreary. And these two wonderful people here are my family." Mrs. McCreary said as she pointed from T. Thomas to Dorothy one after the other as she introduced them both. "This handsome gentleman here is my husband T. Thomas. And the lovely auburn-colored red head with the amazing green eyes is our daughter, Dorothy. Isn't she just adorable?" Mrs. Ida B. McCreary playfully asked while embarrassingly pinching her daughter's cheek. As Potential hypnotically nodded his head yes as he answered Mrs. Ida B. McCreary's question, looking as if he was actually on the verge of slobbering.

Talent, who was the most outspoken of the two, plus a little bit embarrassed now from her brother's child-like antics, kindly took it upon herself to respond. She frustratingly cut her eyes at Potential, who was still staring at Dorothy in pure amazement. "Hello Mr. and Mrs. McCreary. Hello, Dorothy. My name is Talent, and this knuckle-head little joker here is my brother, Potential," Talent respectfully stated. She nudged Potential as hard as she could with her elbow in hopes of knocking him down.

"What!" Potential irritably stated, upset at the fact that Talent had actually ruined his current thought process as he quickly punched her and ran, dodging an elderly woman's wheelchair as he took off.

"Why you little…!" Talent barked instantly giving chase knowing in her mind that she wouldn't possibly catch him. She never could catch him but still, she thought it was worth a try as she rapidly maneuvered around a teenage couple and their child in high pursuit.

The adults stood around enjoying one another's company while laughing at Talent and Potential bicker about one thing or the other. But no one seemed to be paying attention to the occupant of the grey Mercury sedan that was parked only a short distance away, taking pictures, capturing them all with every pose.

For years the occupant of the sedan had patiently awaited the perfect opportunity to destroy the McCreary's life for the embarrassment they caused several years prior when they actually chose to allow Meharry hospital, and this so-called ophthalmologist Dr.

Wiseman, to perform their eye procedures. A procedure that was rightfully theirs, or so the occupant thought. Resentment was felt by many around them. But it was the occupant who took it the most personal.

And the very thought of that act alone was enough to cause their resentment towards the McCreary's to reach a level that was almost impossible for them to control.

They violently gripped and snatched on the steering wheel of their vehicle as if they were about to pull it off. Breathing erratically while constantly drooling, they started talking to themselves, "calm down! Remember, you must remain calm, if not you're going to blow it. And we've come too far to lose it all now. So, get it together!" The occupant reasoned with themselves, in 3rd person, steadily eyeing the family they had come to despise so bitterly, both mentally and physically. While realizing that the many photographs they had taken of the McCreary's were now spewed all over the front seat and floorboards of the vehicle.

They started collecting the pictures while stacking them into four different piles according to their dates. The occupant then slid their hand across the chrome metal object that snugly lay pressed against their thigh, caressing it as if it were some types of animal. The cold hard steel caused a strong sense of euphoria to run deep within them, one that was better than anything they had actually experienced before. Better than money or any other achievement that they had received in their lives. And the best was yet to come, so the occupant thought.

Sadistically fantasizing about the day that they finally got the opportunity to use the piece of steel in which they'd become so acquainted with over the years. "In due time my love, in due time," the occupant promised, conversing with the chrome metal object with a devilish grin.

Feeling the powerful effects of their invisibility, the occupant then exited the vehicle heading toward the crowd of people that talked and laughed so aimlessly as if they had not a care in the world. The occupant kept walking until they were directly behind the crowd of people. They smelled the sweet aroma of the McCreary's fragrance and the freshness of their hair as they stood within arm's reach of them acting as if they were taking pictures of a young teen couple and their child.

Unable to resist, the occupant then reached out and gently caressed a strand of Dorothy's long, auburn colored mane, taking another deep whiff, bringing their face within an inch or two of Dorothy's head without any detection.

Sensing a negative vibe from somewhere close behind them, T. Thomas and Mrs. Ida B. McCreary both turned around in order to check their surroundings. But nothing was there except for the teen couple and their child, a few older pedestrians that were headed into the hospital, and an odd-looking doctor wearing a short white lab coat who was now climbing into a grey Mercury sedan holding in their hand some type of chrome-looking, metal object. The same object that they had just used to sever off several strands of Dorothy and

Mrs. Ida B. McCreary's hair, along with a small piece of T. Thomas' sleeve.

Smiling broadly now, the occupant stored the items into a large zip-lock bag labeled "evidence." Then they slowly pulled away from the curb watching the McCreary's through their rearview mirror the entire way until finally making a right turn on D. B. Todd Blvd.

"Making you suffer is going to be my pleasure, McCreary's. And suffer you will! Suffer... You... Most... Definitely... Will!" The occupant sacredly vowed releasing a very loud and obnoxious bout of demented laughter as they casually cruised along. "Aahhh ha ha ha ha! Aaahhhh ha ha ha haaa!"

Chapter 28

A month or so had passed before Shica and Sheena finally conjured up the perfect plan for Liz's payback. And they would serve it to her cold; the only true way for their revenge to be issued out after such heinous acts of betrayal, they thought.

Liz's behavior was completely unacceptable, and she had to be taught a lesson for it. One that would hopefully open up her eyes and cause her to drift from her devious ways.

Shica and Sheena had wrestled with several different options pertaining to what they would actually do to her. Because even though Liz was a handful at times with her deceptive ways, she was still their friend and they both loved her. But they knew right was right and wrong was wrong, and what Liz was actually trying to do to her little cousin Talent was definitely sin. One that neither of them could possibly live with if they allowed it to happen, which they would not, especially if they could help.

So, they made sure to avoid Liz just long enough for her not to become suspicious of them. As they continuously gave her the false belief that they were all still as cool as they had once been. But portraying as if all was good was extremely difficult to do at times due to her rude and disrespectful ways.

The more they viewed Liz from afar, the more apparent Liz's intentions had become to them. Which served no one, other than herself, any good at all, and only made it that much easier for Shica and Sheena to execute their plan.

Sheena's basement was the place where they both decided to carry out Liz's punishment. Since her mother worked long consistent hours during the day, it would definitely give them more than enough time to administer the pain that they both felt Liz deserved. And even more time to clean up the mess they would make if it actually came to that. How much of a mess would solely be up to Liz and the resistance that she showed towards what they were about to do.

Although, they had no real intentions of hurting her, they knew in the back of their minds that it was a very strong possibility that they might have to. Because Liz had never been the type of person to go down without a fight. And fight she would do to the end. Or at least until somebody submitted. And more than likely that somebody was not going to be her. Shica and Sheena knew that for a fact, so they prepared for it by all means.

Arranging the furniture of the basement in order to make it more spacious by Shica and Sheena, transferring all breakable objects to the far end wall. They were preparing just in case a struggle occurred so the valuables of Sheena's home would not be destroyed.

And Sheena's mom would still be completely clueless as to what had actually transpired.

They surveyed the room with a feeling of pure satisfaction before strategically implementing the last and final stages of their plan as they laid plastic across the basement's hardwood floor. And the loud rustling sounds of the unraveling plastic almost caused them both to lose their nerve.

What had once been planned as a simple scare tactic or possible beat down of a so-called friend, was now beginning to look like an assassin's crime scene from a mafia movie. And Shica didn't like that one bit, nor did her conscience.

Who are you to impart judgement or carry out vengeance on my behalf? Vengeance is mine – And mine alone! I shall repay! The deep voice angrily stated as a strong gust of wind instantly swept throughout the downstairs basement vehemently blowing the curtains from the windows.

Feeling the cold breeze, but unaware if she had actually heard the voice or not, Shica hurriedly asked Sheena to place the call.

She dialed the number and the phone started to ring. Liz answered on the third ring, "Hello."

Sheena notified Shica that she was now on the line, gesturing to her what she should do next.

"Talk! Duh!" Shica irritably whispered back in return.

Sheena started the conversation with small talk. Shica laughed and joked around in the background making it seem as if they were having the time of their lives. Knowing that it was almost impossible for their friend to miss out on a good time. Liz instantly became overly excited.

"Hold up! What y'all doing over there?" Liz anxiously exclaimed as she hobbled from one end of the room to the other in search of her missing sandal while cradling the phone with her shoulder.

"Just hanging out."

Liz lifted both ends of the couch, only to find nothing there. "Arrrgghh!" She frustratingly hissed, spinning around in a complete circle. When she stopped turning there it was wedged underneath the corner of the living room table. "How did my shoe... You know what, nevermind!" Liz laughed shaking her head as she hurriedly slapped her shoe onto her foot and quickly made her exit. She totally forgot that Sheena was on the phone.

"Worked like a charm," Sheena stated with a wink.

"I knew it would," Shica confidently replied. "Now get in position! We don't have a lot of time," she demanded as they both sprang into action in order to carry out the next phase of their plan.

Swiftly moving through the neighborhood streets, Liz's mind was consumed with nothing but fun, motivating her legs to walk even faster. She wanted to run but decided against it just in case boys were there. She couldn't imagine herself entering the house drench in sweat. She didn't have a clue that it was actually a set-up. Quickly scaling the steps a few moments later, Liz released a repetitive flurry of knocks on Sheena's front door.

Knock... Knock... Knock... Knock...

"You ready?" Shica quietly asked Sheena in muffled speech.

Sheena shook her head in agreement and instantly placed her hand on the doorknob in order to allow Liz access inside of the home.

"Well, let's do it!" Shica whispered, quickly finding her hiding spot behind the bathroom door patiently waiting for Liz to pass so that she could sneak up on her from behind.

Counting to three, Sheena opened the door with a huge smile on her face.

As Liz rudely brushed past her without an acknowledgement of any kind. She headed straight toward the basement where the loud music blared from the stereo's sound system at high-volume.

"Evil wench!" Sheena spat in a low raspy voice shaking her head in disbelief as she closed the door behind her disrespectful friend. She locked the door then made her way toward the staircase as well.

"Ooohh, yeeahh! That's my song!" Liz loudly yelled sauntering down the basement steps with her arms flaring high above her head only to find it empty. "Where is everybody?" Liz asked in bewilderment.

And those were the last words she remembered speaking before feeling the hard shove from behind her and seeing the bright flashes of a very intense light coming from somewhere underneath her eyelids.

Knowing that Liz's mind would be elsewhere when she first entered the room, Shica and Sheena took full advantage of the opportunity. They placed a wooden block at the bottom of the stairs to force Liz off of her feet, knowing that she would trip and fall because of it. They used the block instead of exerting all of the unnecessary energy that it would take in trying to wrestle her down themselves and possibly losing the battle, which they definitely could not afford. But their plan worked perfectly.

As soon as Liz's body hit the pavement, Sheena quickly struck her with the rubber-like baton that she kept concealed in the small of her back giving her no chance at all of regaining her balance.

After administering the first blow, Sheena was surprised that she did not want to stop, and that scared her. She never realized how much she disliked Liz until that very moment.

Recognizing the crazed look that was now in Sheena's eyes, Shica slowly pried the tightly gripped baton from her hand. She thought to herself that she would definitely have to keep a closer eye on Sheena from that point on. Because she knew that if she didn't, Sheena would possibly hurt Liz and hurt her bad. And Shica definitely wasn't trying to deal with that type of situation.

They bound her hands behind her back before swiftly lifting her to her feet. Shica placed Liz in a worn chair that sat in the center of the floor. And with a gagged mouth, Liz bucked like a wild bull that was trying to break free. But it was no use. The scarves had been tied too tight and Liz's fight began a little too late for it to be effective in any type of way. And for the first time in her young life, Liz's body quivered with fear. Her fear caused her to release a stream of urine that ran down the inside of her legs.

She started to plead for mercy with her eyes. The embarrassment that Liz currently displayed was actually heartfelt. At least to Shica it was. Sheena on the other hand wasn't convinced. But she did show a small sense of compassion when she wiped her down, cleaning up the puddle of urine that had now formed around her feet.

Liz had done some very horrible and low-down things to people over the years. And even when Shica and Sheena really didn't want to assist her in them, they did. Sometimes out of fear, other times because of their loyalty to their so-called friendship.

But Liz had never really been a friend to anyone, Sheena thought. Not even to her little cousin Talent who loved her dearly.

Talent had no knowledge regarding all the things that Liz had actually tried to do to her over the years, or so they thought. And for the longest time, even they were deceived themselves. Liz had always made it seem as if she was doing the things that she did to Talent to help toughen her up. But that wasn't the case at all. And the letter that Shica and Sheena received from Liz clearly showed it.

It seemed as if Liz was actually trying to destroy Talents life forever. She tried to use them in order to do her dirty work, which only infuriated Sheena even more. *But, not this time*, Sheena thought as she angrily snatched the phone from the receiver. But this time placing a call to Talent.

"Hello."

"Yes, may I speak to Talent, please?" Sheena whined.

"This is she."

"Talent! Please hurry! I really need your help. I don't know what to do!" Sheena hysterically yelled hanging up the phone before Talent could respond.

Shica was standing not too far away, closely observing her friend's theatrics. When she hung up the phone, Shica instantly began clapping her hands. "And the best female actress of the year goes to," Shica said in a very animated voice. "Sheena Snillum!" she loudly announced faking the loud cheers of an applauding crowd. She started shaking her head but was smirking the entire time. "Girl, I have seen so many different sides of you today that even I don't really know who you are anymore." Shica said giggling.

"Well, I guess that makes two of us then, doesn't it? Honestly, I thought you were someone totally different as well. So maybe it's fair to say that we don't know each other as well as we thought we did huh?" Sheena sarcastically stated.

As she turned and headed back up the stairs, she left Shica to ponder on her words.

Chapter 29

Sheena's phone call had Talent hysterical and somewhat discombobulated. Feeling a strong sense of Deja vu, Talent rushed from her house as fast as she could. Just hours earlier she witnessed her big cousin Liz do the same thing as well.

The constant queasiness in Talent's gut was warning her that something wasn't right. But ignoring her gut feeling, she continued heading in Sheena's direction. She broke into a slow jog to help get there even quicker. "Lord, watch over me for I know not what's ahead. But I know in your hands I am safe," Talent silently prayed. Leaping the steps of Sheena's home two at a time, Talent impatiently knocked on the front door.

Knock... Knock... Knock... Knock...

She could hear the music blaring from somewhere within the home. Thinking that no one could hear her, she decided to knock a little harder.

Knock... Knock... Knock... Knock...

But still, no one answered. When no one answered the door, it almost sent her into a complete state of panic. Knowing that someone was definitely inside, Talent did all that she could do to get a visual. She tried to look through the windows, but the dark color of

Sheena's living room window wouldn't permit it. "Dang!" Talent fretted.

Talent paced back and forth multiple times before deciding to check the back of the house. As she walked towards the back, she was almost attacked by the neighbor's dog. She never once thought to look through the small basement window that she passed along the way. If she had, for the first time in Talent's life, she would have recognized Liz's fear.

Still unable to gain access inside of the home, Talent wondered if maybe she should go for help. Thinking for a moment, she decided against it as a faint voice from within whispered for her to check the locks.

Running as fast as could back to the front of the house, Talent dashed up the steps and gave it a twist. She quickly regained her balance after stumbling from the unexpected opening of the door. "Thank you, Lord!" Talent expressed. As she cautiously pushed open the door, she was totally unaware of what awaited her on the other side. But she could definitely feel the strong sense of trouble lurking somewhere deep within the shadows.

Being as quiet as she could be, Talent scanned her surrounding in search of a weapon, preferably something small and sharp. And that's when she spotted Sheena at the counter of her mother's kitchen pouring herself a glass of water from an extremely large container.

The tears that Sheena previously used in order to lure Talent to her house were now completely gone, leaving Talent wondering if the tears had ever been real. Upon seeing Sheena's changed expression, Talent's anger increased instantly. "Sheena, where is my cousin! And you better not lie to me either!" Talent barked through clinched teeth menacingly, scowling at Sheena as if she were waiting for her to say the wrong thing.

Nervously spitting water all over the kitchen counter, Sheena fought hard to find the proper words in hopes of diffusing the ticking time-bomb that currently stood before her. "Talent! How did you...?" Sheena began quickly bringing herself to an abrupt stop after noticing Talent's seriousness go from cold to extremely venomous in a mere matter of seconds.

"Never mind how I've done anything!" Talent aggressively responded. "Just take me to my cousin and take me to her now!" she barked sending a strong streak of fear coursing down Sheena's spine.

She hurriedly led Talent down the basement stairs babbling the entire way, doing all she could to warn Shica that Talent was now amongst them. Sheena tried to use her conversation as a distraction, speaking louder and louder with each and every step.

But to no avail, Shica heeded not a single word of it due to the extremely loud music playing. It wasn't until Shica actually laid eyes on Talent that she hurriedly shut it off.

She recognized her cousin Liz's muffled cries for help violently echoing throughout the almost empty room. And from the look in Talent's eyes, you could definitely tell that she was very upset as she gripped the metal letter-opener that she kept concealed in her front pocket that she picked up from the living room table.

Looking into Talent's face, Shica and Sheena could see that she was completely emotionless. Talent's face was as hard as granite stone. The same as it had been when she defended herself against the bully at school.

As she quietly made her way over to her cousin Liz to untie her from the old rickety chair, she noticed for the first time the plastic covered floor. "What the....!" Talent exclaimed wishing that looks could kill. Seething with rage, Talent instantly kneeled in front of Liz in order to contain herself, doodling something on the plastic, as if she was writing while mumbling incoherent words to herself that had the familiarity of a prayer.

And a prayer it actually was.

The entire scene sort of reminded her of when the Pharisee's brought the adulterous woman to Jesus. Testing him that they might have something of which to accuse him.

As Shica and Sheena went on and on about all of the deceitful things that Liz had done to Talent or had tried to do, like they did to Jesus, Talent kept right on doodling. It wasn't until they completely finished their ranting that Talent finally stood to her feet.

"He who is without sin among you, let them cast the first stone," Talent boldly stated looking them directly in their eyes as she quoted the same exact scripture that Jesus quoted to the Pharisee's after they spoke of stoning the adulterous woman.

And just like the Pharisee's, who had begun to disappear one at a time until no one remained but the adulteress, Talent's words hit Shica and Sheena like a jab from a professional boxer knocking them both backwards until their backs pressed flatly against the basement's wall.

Their legs were as limp as noodles now, and the only reason that they hadn't fallen completely on their behinds was because of the furniture that they placed against the wall earlier that day in which they were grateful that they had. The conviction they felt pierced their hearts like a double-edge sword cutting and slicing them from every direction until they finally landed on their knees in prayer. They sincerely started asking for God's forgiveness.

"Who are you to impart judgement or carry out vengeance on my behalf," Talent said pointing her finger in the face of Shica who now seemed terrified. Having no idea that those were the same exact words that had been spoken to Shica earlier. And the very same words that Shica had denied hearing before.

But there was no denying them now because God had spoken to her yet again. But this time, it was through the deliverance of Talent.

After reprimanding Shica and Sheena, Talent then focused her undivided attention on Liz who was now squirming in her chair constantly pleading with her eyes to be released. "For several years now, you've done nothing at all but try and bring harm to me. And with every attempt, you've failed causing you only to hate me even more." Talent said. "And I've been aware of it all, since the beginning."

She told Liz about the things she knew about. "From the decapitating of my dolls when we were younger, all the way to the first day of this school year, where you coerced those girls to gang me in the hallway," Talent venomously spat masking her anger. She lifted Liz's head back to an upright position with the knuckle of her fist so that they would remain eye to eye. "And through all of your deceitfulness, I've continuously loved you," Talent told her. "Not because you deserve it, but because God has continuously given me the strength to do so," she said.

Then like the scene from the movie "The Godfather" when Michael Corleone grabbed his brother Fredo's face before aggressively kissing him on the cheek after his unbelievable act of betrayal towards him and the family, which symbolized the "kiss of death," Talent did Liz the exact same way. "No weapon that you will ever form against me shall prosper," Talent confidently told Liz.

She looked her square in the eyes before turning and walking away, continuously thanking God once again for giving her the strength not to repay evil for evil as she left her sitting exactly where she was.

But before leaving she turned back to her cousin one more time, "I bet you wasn't expecting me to do something like that, were you cousin?" Talent said with a forced smile, repeating the exact same words that Liz had spoken to her after her altercation with the bully before turning to head up the stairs and out of each of their lives for good.

Chapter 30

The day had finally arrived for Talent to visit the campus of FCA and the excitement of it all had her nerves in a complete uproar. She changed clothes at least twenty different times, and after an hour or so, she still hadn't decided on what she should wear.

"What's wrong with me?" Talent asked as she flung another outfit on top of the already highly stacked pile of clothing that now formed at the foot of her bed. Still rummaging through her closet, Talent finally made a decision. She picked out a white polo style, short sleeve shirt, some beige khaki capri pants, and her brown leather loafers with the matching belt. "Wow, after all that, this is what I come up with, huh?" Talent laughed looking at herself in the mirror as she combed through her hair.

"Talent, let's get a move on before you make us late!" Survivor screamed double checking herself in the mirror making sure her attire was immaculate. She was striking several different poses to make sure she was sure about her outfit.

Mrs. B. Lee was standing in the doorway witnessing the entire act, shaking her head in disbelief. "May the Lord help you chile and help you quickly. Because if not, then that big, inflated head of yours is just gon' up and float away someday leaving you completely brainless." Mrs. B. Lee said laughing at her daughter who was striking even more poses now than before as Potential and Talent joined in on the fun.

With Talent and Potential right by Survivor's side, Big John played the role of photographer catching every single pose with his imaginary camera.

The photo shoot went on for a minute or so, before it finally came to an end as each member of the Clifton family erupted in good-hearted laughter, tightly embracing one another as they did.

"Watch it now old timer," Talent playfully told her grandfather using her hand as a guard to protect her hair from his oversized arm, that had accidentally brushed up against her head. "Look, I love you and all, but I'll fight an old man for messing up my hair," Talent stated. "Especially when it took as long as it did for me to do," she said animatedly bouncing around like Muhammad Ali, throwing jab after jab while quickly shuffling her feet.

"Whoa now champ!" Big John said back pedaling and showing a little footwork of his own. "I don't want *noooo* trouble," he stated smiling at Talent who was the spitting image of her mother, just lighter.

And letting Big John off with a simple warning, Talent smiled and hugged her grandfather's neck placing a huge kiss on his right cheek before playfully punching him in the stomach.

I have such an incredible family, Big John thought to himself as he opened the car door for all the beautiful women in his life. Then he playfully scrubbed the head of his grandson Potential, smiling as he entered the vehicle himself. *I want to thank you Lord for all the many blessings that you have bestowed upon me*, Big John silently prayed as he placed the car in drive, slowly pulling away from the curb, guiding the big sedan toward Florine Cowan Academy. Better known as FCA.

Chapter 31

The scenery was magnificent. One that neither of them had ever experienced before in the inner city. The grass was greener. The air was cleaner. And the trees that aligned the long winding driveway looked like something that they had only seen on television. And they were enlightened to know that it was all owned by blacks. That fact alone made the scenery even more mesmerizing.

Florine Cowan was the daughter of a slave who received the early beginning of her teachings from the slave master's daughter, Ms. Suzie Mae Whitehouse, who in which, deemed her completely incapable of learning due to the color of her skin.

As a young child, Suzie Mae received the notion from the adult whites of her household that no matter how hard she tried reading, teaching, or attempting either in any way, to show the blacks of their land any type of educational curriculum was impossible for them to discern due to the smallness of their brains.

And she believed it, which years later, Florine would prove the entire Whitehouse family wrong after she graduated valedictorian of her class, receiving an even higher IQ test score than Ms. Suzie Mae herself.

She battled racism throughout her entire life as a student in the Nashville area. And once an adult, Florine dedicated majority of her time elevating as many of her people as she possibly could, which eventually led to the opening of FCA several years later. Which to current date is still one of the most prominent schools in the entire Metro Davidson County area by far.

And Talent would have the opportunity to attend this well renowned historically African American school of advancement for colored people if in fact she decided to do so.

FCA was one of three major schools established by African Americans. Another was Mrs. Mary McLeod Bethune's school in Daytona. Her school was a private industrial school for Negro girls established in 1904, which later became Bethune-Cookman, a fully accredited coeducational college started in 1943.

And the third school was Booker T. Washington's Tuskegee Institute. The school which changed the entire history of agriculture and science forever, especially in the south. This was due to the brilliant mind of Dr. George Washington Carver, better known to the world as the "Peanut Man."

Completely flabbergasted from the welcoming they received, the Clifton's were at a loss for words as they ogled over the huge band that was playing and the brilliantly painted "Welcome to FCA" banner that was created by a few of the students.

"This is one beautiful place!" Big John said in amazement as he slowly took in all of his surroundings, viewing nothing but a sea of black faces, a visual that he would etch into his mind forever.

The recruiter's allowed the Clifton's the opportunity to absorb all the beautiful qualities that they had come to love themselves, about the establishment as they patiently awaited them on the lawn.

Afterwards, they handed each of Talent's family members the correct visiting pass without making one mistake.

"How did you know who I was, young man?" Grandma Clifton flirtatiously asked.

Smiling at the gentlemen that had just given her the pass as if she were surprised.

"Momma, stop it! Please, don't start!" Mrs. B. Lee said to her mother who was obviously flirting with the young man standing before them. As the rest of the Clifton family laughed realizing that it was going to be a good day.

"Don't start what!" Grandma Clifton said defiantly before rolling her eyes. "Look here lil girl, I may be old but I'm not in my grave yet! And I definitely know fine when I see it. So, truth be told, this young Negro right here, *IS GORGEOUS*! So, ease back and let a seasoned woman handle her business!" Grandma Clifton said grinning from ear to ear as she placed her hand on the recruiter's bicep and purred like a kitten, while slightly adjusting her wig with a wink.

Upon seeing this, everybody burst into laughter, even the students that were currently holding the "Welcome to FCA" banner. Especially when Grandma Clifton shifted legs showing off more of her fully round frame and handing the recruiter a piece of paper as if it were her phone number.

"Call me sometimes big boy. Who knows, maybe we can have a little fun," she said flirtatiously before strolling away with a twist, knocking the other recruiter off balance with a bump of her hip.

The recruiter was at a complete loss of words and didn't know what to do. And the flustered look upon his face described exactly what it was that he was feeling at the moment, which was definitely a mass of total confusion. "Is she serious?" the recruiter nervously asked.

Instantly recognizing the opportunity for another good round of laughter, Potential approached the recruiter with a smile, tugging on his shirt sleeve in order to get his attention. "Look here Mr., don't worry about it. All Grandma really wants is a kiss. So, the quicker you kiss her, the quicker you can get it over with. But let me advise you of something though. She normally gets a little rowdy if she doesn't feel a little tongue. So, trust me, make it a good one," Potential said snickering before casually walking away laughing underneath his breath while patiently awaiting the explosion.

"Tongue! Wh... wh... what do you mean, tongue?" The recruiter shouted looking at Potential who was now shrugging his shoulders as if he were crazy.

Potential quickly turned his head.

"Look, I'm not trying to be disrespectful or anything and Lord knows that I love my job," the recruiter said. "But I'll be darned if I'm tongue kissing Grandma Clifton in order to keep it!" He stated seriously searching the surrounding area for an exit just in case he had to make a quick break for it. As he eased the lankiness of his long frame towards a small space that was between Talent and Potential, making sure to steer clear of Grandma Clifton and her full-sized lips.

Realizing that the recruiter was about to dash at any given moment, Talent sadly brought the joke to an end. "Alright now you guys, I think he's suffered enough," Talent professed grabbing hold of the recruiter's arm to keep him from bolting away. She tried to alleviate his anxieties with a smile. But honestly, that wasn't working either. "Welcome to the Clifton's, Mr. recruiter. Now aren't we just amazing?" Talent said.

As big John walked by patting him on the back, steadily laughing before making a small comment on his own. "Let's get a move on youngster before these old bunions of mine get to acting up on me. As you can see, I'm not as young as I used to be, and neither are they!" Big John whispered tilting his head towards Mrs. B. Lee and Grandma Clifton while steadily walking in the direction of the beautifully manicured building called Dr. Roy Lee Hall.

Relieved that it was only a joke, the recruiter felt as if a huge weight had been lifted off his shoulders. He had no idea what he would have done if he had actually lost his job. Exhaling deeply and smoothing out the wrinkles that formulated in his clothes from perspiration, he started to catch up with his partner who was now entering FCA's highly modernized gymnasium.

The tour was flying by like a breeze and the Clifton's couldn't believe how much the campus of FCA actually looked like that of a college. All the different education departments had their own private buildings which were named after famous African American abolitionist. And covering much of the minor details about the school's history and artifacts, the recruiters then decided on heading to the cafeteria for lunch where they all ate fried chicken, macaroni and cheese, baked apples, collard greens and a very delicious piece of pecan pie, washing it down with a large glass of home-made sweet tea.

They ate and laughed while enjoying one another's company to the utmost. While the Dean, along with the assistant Principal, who just so happened to be his twin brother, decided to join them as well.

Dr. J. L. Lewis and his brother grew up in the rough and rugged parts of north Nashville in a housing development called "John Henry Hale." Although extremely poverty-stricken, sharing the cramped confines of a small three-bedroom housing project with six of their other siblings, The Lewis' brothers still managed to avoid the many dangerous pitfalls that came with inner-city living. They pulled themselves out of the ghetto by their bootstraps which took nothing but pure determination and a lot of faith in God.

Upon their success, the Lewis' brothers were making every effort to do the same for every enabled or disadvantaged African American descendant that they possibly could. They created one of the most highly successful programs for the so-called under privileged child of color to finally have the opportunity to receive a higher education with no capital needed as long as they maintained the grades. And Talent was now about to be a beneficiary of this extremely amazing opportunity.

So, congratulating Talent on all of her many accomplishments and wishing her family well, the Lewis' brothers shook each of their hands before arranging to make their departure. "Well family, it's been an honor sharing time with you. I can't begin to tell you how much I truly enjoyed myself. Honestly, I haven't laughed this hard in years," Dr. J. L. Lewis said thinking back to the days when he and his family use to congregate after church and enjoy one another's company, all while laughing and stuffing their bellies with some of their mother's good home-cooked food.

Dr. J. L. Lewis held the door open for his brother to exit. But not before saying good-bye himself. "Now remember Potential, I'm expecting you to come here as well. So, make sure you keep those grades up you hear me? And in a few more years I'm going to send for you too," Dr. J. L. Lewis stated in all seriousness. As he waved goodbye to the family, leaving Potential with a huge smile on his face, feeling like the luckiest little guy in the world.

And honestly, finally exiting the cafeteria themselves, the recruiters saved the best and final part of the tour for last, which was their state-of-the-art award winning African American museum.

Chapter 32

The building was as big as The Parthenon of Centennial Park and constructed with the same type of style and elegance.

Big John couldn't wait to step foot inside of it. Although he had dropped out of school at an early age himself, Big John never lost the passion for reading and learning about the heritage of his people and couldn't wait to pass his knowledge along to one of the only other male members of the Clifton family, his grandson Potential, whom he instantly pulled closer to him as they both entered the building.

The marbled floors were waxed and polished like that of a ballroom's dance hall. As each of the Clifton's reflections vividly shone back at them as they stared down into the glistening surface, giving each of them the feeling as if they were actually walking on ice.

The windows were covered with designs from what had to be one of the most talented artists to ever pick up a paint brush who the Clifton's later found out was a local talent from the very city of Nashville himself named Terrance Le'mont London. Which also, in fact, amazed them all. Living in the city of Nashville most of their lives, if not all, the Clifton's had no idea that this type of history even existed. And the recruiters were incredible in their passionate way of explaining it to them.

So, as they delved through fact after fact about one historical figure to another, Big John's focus remained on Henry "Box" Brown, who received his freedom by mailing himself by crate from the slave infested state of Virginia to the free lands of Philadelphia, Pennsylvania, by boxing himself up as cargo. Where he stored more than enough food for the twenty-seven-hour journey with the assistance of James C. A. Smith, a free black man, and Samuel A. Smith, a Caucasian shoemaker who placed a "dry goods" sticker on the outside of the box and also made the arrangements of shipping Henry to the office of Quaker Merchant Passmore Williamson, another reliable and very dependable source of friends.

As Big John described in intricate detail Henry "Box" Brown's amazing escape to freedom, Potential could hardly believe his ears and hung onto his grandfather's every word in pure astonishment. He wondered how a man that was prohibited from reading and writing could possibly plan something so spectacularly genius and actually get away with it.

As the words of Grandma Clifton instantly entered his mind. "All things are possible with God," Grandma Clifton would religiously quote. As Potential repeated the words underneath his breath while following his grandfather to another famous and very courageous abolitionist by the name of Gabrielle Prosser.

"Prosser, who although was unsuccessful in the leading of his early 1800's slave revolt against the whites of Richmond, Virginia due to the betrayal from another fellow slave exposing his plans, still captured America's undivided attention with this very courageous act in hopes of retrieving his freedom. And is still glorified as a martyr amongst our people until this very day," the recruiter stated as Potential stared at the pictures that hung before him in awe, secretly comparing the features of his ancestors to that of himself.

The wide nose, full lips and the extremely powerful bone structure in their features, Potential possessed as well, along with the very same muscular physique. Which sent a feeling of pride traveling throughout the course of his entire body as he beamed proudly. He held his head up higher, poking out what little of a chest he had at the time even further, and did everything in his power to try and mimic the strengthened posture, of all the heroic figures that currently surrounded him.

Witnessing the reaction of his grandson made Big John proud. He was remembering the time that he himself felt the exact same way upon receiving the enlightenment of who he really was as a black man, and from where and what type of incredible people that he had actually come, finally giving him the ability to sift through the lies that society constantly tried to thrust upon him as an African American male.

And Potential would now have the opportunity to do the same. The confliction between truth and lies tugged at the inner most-deepest parts of Potential's young anatomy, suddenly drifting him into a world of mass confusion as he tried his best to decipher the different emotions without giving into his still very immature understanding. Although he felt joy, happiness, strength and courage, anger still loomed within him as well. And honestly, Potential didn't know why?

Never realizing that it was the spiritual connection that linked him to men such as Henry "Box" Brown, Gabrielle Prosser, Denmark Vessey, Nat Turner and all the many other African American patriots that fought, died, marched, and shed their blood to help bring justice and equality to the black men here in America. But in their attempts of doing so, they were savagely beaten, killed, maimed, and even hanged. Potential's breathing became erratic as he gradually moved through the museum, retaining every word that was being expressed to him by his grandfather and recruiter's alike about the early beginnings of his ancestor's and their cruel and very disturbing experiences here in this country.

And watching the tormenting truth slowly eat away at his grandson's young soul, Big John sat back and allowed Potential to take it all in without saying a word. "This he needs," Big John reasoned amongst himself, keeping a close eye on Potential's very distraught state-of-mind, knowing that he would eventually bring balance to the young man's mental anguish by teaching him exactly how to channel all those negative feelings into something extremely more powerful over time.

He would teach him so he would become victorious over his hatred and not just another statistic of America's vicious and very biased penal system where there were currently over two million people enslaved within the systems walls and more than forty percent of them being black.

It was statistics such as this that Big John feared most. He knew exactly how it felt to be a target. Because he, himself, had been a target since the very first day that he exited his mother's womb in this so-called land of the free as well. But in his opinion, that quote didn't consider black folks at all.

Big John's suffering had been immensely severe growing up in the south. He lived during a time where lynching's, beatings, rapes, and bombings of innocent churches were all normal. And although times had drastically changed for the better, racism hadn't. It had only disguised itself under a new name, "the judicial system," where blacks still received harsher punishments, mainly because of the color of their skin, more so than from actually committing the crime which big John swore that Potential would never be a part of. As he looked up from his grandson's perturbed face and witnessed the beautiful big brown eyes of Emmett Till staring down upon him. "Be sure to protect him, Big John. Make sure that you protect him," Big John heard him whisper.

It was the eyes of Emmett Till that brought the horrible events of his young innocent life instantly flooding back to the full front of his mind. As the images of Emmett's disfigured appearance once again flashed before Big John's eyes, causing him to recoil. All of a sudden it was 1955 all over again and big John was seated in the living room amongst his family reading a magazine when he came across a picture so gruesome it made him drop the book entirely. A picture of Emmett Louis Till's deceased body.

A beautiful, strong young African American male from Chicago, Illinois who tragically lost his life at the tender age of fourteen in the racist city of Money – Mississippi, for allegedly whistling at a white woman.

Although Emmett Till's trial received national and international coverage from the press, and lasted a total of five full days, which might I add was a world record in Mississippi for a black man, at the time, the culprits who were responsible for his murder were found not guilty, and it only took the jury no longer than an hour to decide their fate. Which caused many African American communities all across the country to respond with anger, with Big John and his family being one of them.

Rehashing these brutal events still held the same effect on him now that they did back when he was only a child. A very strong sense of unhealthy, but controllable anger rushed his normally calm demeanor, sending a single tear stubbornly streaming from his eye. He aggressively wiped his face with the palm of his huge, calloused hand as if he was trying to eradicate the thoughts from his mind forever. And with anger in his heart, Big John began to pray.

Grabbing Potential's hand and pulling him down into a kneeling position in the presence of all of their ancestor's and family members alike, he constantly asked his Lord and Savior, Jesus Christ for his profound provision.

And kneeling beside his grandfather, but never closing his eyes, nor bowing his head as the others had done, Potential felt that prayer was purposeless. After all, it had never stopped the atrocious acts of southern whites from taking the lives of all the many innocent men, women and children that hung on the wall before him, had it? And it definitely wouldn't stop them from trying to take his, he sadly thought to himself.

Knowing after today's visit to FCA's amazing African American museum, he would never again be the same.

Finally exiting the museum's doors with Big John's arm flung around his tiny, little shoulders as he slightly shielded his eyes from the brightness of the sun, Potential's resentment grew even stronger as he noticed the two white detectives that was standing at the bottom of the steps making a request for his sister.

"Talent Clifton, we would like to ask you a few questions concerning the kidnapping and aggravated assault of an, uuummm……," the short stubby detective hesitated while looking over the documents that he held clinched between his chubby little fingers. Finding what he was looking for he continued, "an Elizabeth Clifton," he confusingly stated scowling at the papers as if he was actually reading it wrong. But he wasn't. He noticed that they both possessed the same last name and somehow had to be related.

"Elizabeth Clifton!" Grandma Clifton shouted. "Sir, you must be mistaken because Talent and Liz are cousins, and our family ties are tight!" Mrs. B. Lee said with Survivor following suit just as Grandma Clifton fell to her knees, gasping for air from the shock of the news. She was clutching at her chest as if she was having a heart attack, which she quickly realized she was.

"Noooooo!" Potential fearfully screamed, looking into his great grandmother's panic-filled eyes before becoming completely incensed with rage. "This is all your fault! Why don't ya'll just leave us alone!" he aggressively yelled charging the two detectives like a deranged mad man without a weapon, as five loud pops echoed throughout the museum's corridor like fireworks on the 4th of July.

Pop... Pop... Pop... Pop... Pop!

Sending Potential's young body crashing to the pavement in a very awkward position as the entire Clifton family, all except Grandma Clifton, quickly rushed to his side.

"Help me momma, it's hurting me, hurting me badly." Potential weakly whispered before fading into unconsciousness as Survivor hysterically screamed...

"Noooooo!" She yelled pumping furiously on Potential's chest trying her best to revive him... But it was too late, it seemed.